For my 3 *E*s

—S.C.

CHAPTER 1

I hammer the buttons on my controller.

Fireball.

Miss.

Double fireball.

Miss again.

Holy crap, this guy is fast! I can't land anything. "C'mon, Kaigo . . ."

"I know you always play Kaigo, Jaden, but the dragon-cross is only cool if his fireballs actually hit the opponent."

"Thanks, Dev. You want to try?"

I'm in my living room with my friends, Devesh and Hugh. Like most of our gaming sessions, this one started out with us playing each other but ended up with them watching me battle random people online. On screen, two guys in karate gear are beating the crap out of each other.

Fortunately, I've never been in a real-life fight. I wouldn't have a chance. But playing my favorite game, *Cross Ups IV*, I haven't lost a battle in four months. Then again, I've never played against Kn1ght_Rage before.

I whiff another fireball combo when Kn1ght_Rage jumps out of range—again.

"Aw, dude, you almost had him," Hugh says.

"Not even close." As usual, Devesh is keeping it real. "No offense, J, but you're getting owned. Who is this Kn1ght_Rage guy, anyway?"

"I see him online all the time," Hugh says.

Devesh turns to Hugh. "Oh yeah? You ever play him?"

"Once . . . kinda. I left the match before it ended."

"You mean you rage quit." Devesh punches Hugh in the arm.

"No . . ."

"Would you guys shut up? I'm trying to concentrate here."

WHAM! The screen flashes a burst of gold and Kn1ght_Rage's avatar, Blaze, transforms into a phoenix, flapping huge golden wings that send shock waves into me. "How'd he hit me with that Solar Burst? I was blocking!"

"Use your Dragon Breath," Hugh says.

"I will—as soon as I can move again—stupid hit stun! What the . . .?" I drop my move when Kn1ght_ Rage disappears for a second and then reappears, attacking me from behind. "Ugh! I forgot Blaze can teleport. Take that!" I yell as I activate Dragon Breath. Kaigo transforms into a dragon and breathes fire, but my opponent jumps away just in time. "Aaah! I can't get any moves in."

I slam the back button to block the shock waves from the next Solar Burst, but for some reason I still take the punishment. "Why isn't my block working?"

"Look at your Health Meter. You're going to die from chip damage at this rate."

"Shut up, Dev."

"But hey, your Super Meter's full again," Hugh says.

"Yeah, go for it," Devesh says. "But you'd better do some serious damage or it's over."

There's only one move that can get me the win. Kaigo's biggest Super: Dragon Fire.

I hear car doors slamming outside. If that's my mom, I'm so dead. I should turn off the game, but I can't let my streak end like this. Panic makes me go nuts on the controller—a total button mash.

"C'mon . . ."

Miraculously, Kaigo transforms into his dragon side and whirls into a tornado of gray smoke that cuts right through Blaze. Blaze crumples and his Health Meter dives. Now we're both one hit from defeat.

I glance at the clock—6:22 p.m. I don't hear any more noise outside. Maybe it was the neighbors' car? I use my bread-and-butter combo: two crouching light punches back to back, followed by Dragon Claw.

K.O.

"Whaaaaaaat!?!" My friends scream and jump from the couch.

Devesh points to the TV. "The streak continues!"

Hugh throws his hefty form onto the carpet at my feet, bowing and chanting, "You are the master."

"Am I dreaming?" I let the controller drop to the floor. "No, seriously. Am I asleep? Someone hit me."

Devesh and Hugh pile on top of me and pummel me with jabs.

"I've never seen that Super." Hugh settles his glasses back in place.

"That's because I've only ever hit it one time. The timing is crazy hard."

Devesh helps me up off the carpet. "We've got to start streaming your battles. That was godlike!" His phone bings and he pulls it out of his pocket. "I gotta go. I was supposed to meet my dad ten minutes ago. He just texted me from the car in all caps." He grabs his bag and walks backward out of the living room.

"Hold up. I gotta go too, dude. Think your dad will give me a ride?" Hugh grabs his things and runs after Devesh, breathing hard by the time he gets to the end of the hall.

"You live on the other side of town. Why you always asking me for a ride? Train your dad better."

Their voices trail off until the door slams shut behind them.

I'm still staring in disbelief at the TV. My arm muscles twitch like I'm the one who physically battled. Of course, those muscles are scrawny compared to Kaigo's, rippling through his black kung fu uniform. His win quote at the bottom of the screen reads:

"You need more confidence to beat me."

If I looked like that, I'd be confident too.

Just as my thumb descends on the power button, a message pops up on the screen.

Kn1ght_Rage   Tuesday, 6:25 pm
GG JSTAR

Players don't usually message after a fight, unless they're friends. I hesitate but don't want to be rude after the guy complimented me on a good game. I write back:

JStar — Tuesday, 6:27 pm
THNX

Within seconds, another message:

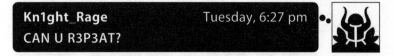

Kn1ght_Rage — Tuesday, 6:27 pm
CAN U R3P3AT?

Can I? I have no idea how I pulled off the Dragon Fire Super. But there's no way I'm going to admit that. I type:

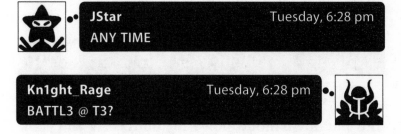

JStar — Tuesday, 6:28 pm
ANY TIME

Kn1ght_Rage — Tuesday, 6:28 pm
BATTL3 @ T3?

My thumbs tap the controller. The Top Tiers Tournament, or T3, is the biggest fighting game tournament in the city. Imagine, competing like Yuudai Sato? That guy is godlike. But there's no way I can compete. With my mom, it's not an option.

I write back:

My curiosity battles with the ticking clock—6:31 p.m. More car doors slam outside. That has to be Mom. Quickly I type:

The answer takes forever. When it finally comes, it just raises more questions.

A key turns in the lock and I automatically go into shutdown mode, powering off the TV and game console and sliding the controller under the cushion next to me. Then I flip open my math book and try to act bored, hoping my mom won't notice my shaking hands.

CHAPTER 2

Y NOT?

Kn1ght_Rage's question pulses in my mind as I listen to my mom starting dinner in the kitchen. I need to think, so I head out the front door. The warm spring air puts me in the mood for ice cream.

Someone's sitting on the swing on the other side of the porch. Cali's wearing a navy T-shirt and jeans. Her long, black hair fluttering in the breeze is the only sign that she's a girl. Her family's house is attached to ours, and we share a huge porch. All the other semi-detached houses on our street have a railing to separate the front porch into two sides. But since Cali and I spent so much time running back and forth to each other's houses when we were little, my dad took down the railing so we wouldn't hurt ourselves climbing over it.

Cali's just sitting there, staring straight ahead like there's a movie screen across the street.

"You okay?" I ask.

"Crappy day," she answers.

"Sunshine's?"

She nods, and we head down our shared front steps and up the street to the local ice cream shop. It's been a while since me and Cali hung out. We're almost the same age, but my December birthday puts me a year ahead of her in school. Now that I'm in grade seven, we don't go to the same school anymore.

Along the way, I tell Cali about Kn1ght_Rage and T3.

"So, what are you gonna do?" she asks.

"Not sure. I really want to go. Man, I wish my mom was normal."

"Your mom *is* normal. She's just a bit over-protective."

"Normal? Don't you remember when she turned off *The Fox and the Hound* because the hunter had a gun? I mean, seriously! It's a Disney movie!"

"She was probably just worried we would be scared."

"We were eleven! It's so stupid. She bans anything

violent for no reason. It's not like watching that stuff actually makes kids fight. I haven't changed since I started playing *Cross Ups*, have I?"

"Well, I haven't seen you much lately . . . how do I know you haven't been beating up little kids for ice cream money?"

"Ha, ha. Anyway, I can't exactly use that as an argument. 'Hey Mom, I've been playing fighting games for years now and there haven't been any negative effects on me.'"

"Yeah, that's not going to work because then there *will* be a negative effect on you." Cali laughs.

"Like my mom beating me!" I take a fake swing at my own face and Cali laughs harder.

"You know, my mom always says your mom's a real tough woman," Cali says. "She says it in this mysterious way—like there's a secret she can't tell me. Maybe your mom used to be a street fighter in the old days."

I try to imagine a young version of Mom, throwing jabs in a back alley in Taipei, but in my mind she's still wearing the black pants and white button-down shirt she wears to work at the diner every day.

The jingling bells on the door let Mrs. Sunshine know we've arrived. I don't know her real name, but that's what we've always called the lady behind the counter. Goosebumps form on our arms when we hit the cold air of the shop. We place our usual orders: strawberry cheesecake for Cali and vanilla for me, and Mrs. Sunshine piles the cones full.

The bells jingle again and my sister, Melanie, comes in with her boyfriend, Roy. She sees Cali at the register paying and her eyes light up. "What's this? You're not even going to pay for Cali's cone? Come on, J, you'll never win her over that way."

"What? So you think I'm going to pay for your cone now?" Roy pulls Melanie to him.

"You always do, babe." Melanie gives him a quick kiss.

My cheeks feel like Kaigo just breathed fire on them. I look over at Cali on the way out of the shop, but there's no reaction on her face.

"Sorry," I say. "You know Melanie."

"No worries." She takes a lick of her ice cream and smiles. "Remember when we were in kindergarten and our moms dressed us up like a bride and groom for Halloween?"

"Yeah. And the next year we were Cinderella and Prince Charming. I only agreed so I could have a sword."

"And you kept poking me with it." She licks her cone thoughtfully. "Wait, were you already playing those video games back then?"

"No, not in grade one. Hey, so playing video games has actually made me *less* violent."

Back in front of our houses, Cali points up. The cherry tree in our shared front yard is full of pink blossoms and the light from the setting sun is making it glow like a Photoshopped picture.

"Hey, you never told me why your day was crappy." I shove the last bit of my cone into my mouth.

"Another time." She dashes up the steps and into her house before I can push for details.

CHAPTER 3

In math class the next day, Mr. Efram writes the problem of the day on the board.

"Yeah," I whisper to Devesh and Hugh, "one invitation to a way cool video game tournament plus two parents who refuse to let you play any violent games. What does that add up to?"

The three of us always work as a group on the problem of the day. Actually, ever since we met each other in math on our first day at Layton, we've done everything together.

"You have to go," Devesh whispers back. "You think Yuudai Sato would back out of a challenge? If you want to be the best, you have to show everyone you can bring it."

"Yeah, maybe if I build a time machine and skip ahead eight months to my birthday." I crumple on my desk. "I looked up the tournament last night.

Since *Cross Ups IV* is 13A, I'd need my parents to come with me and sign a consent form. That's not going to happen."

Mr. Efram finishes writing on the board, runs his hand over his bald spot, and turns to the class. Like every day, he points his thumb to the poster on the wall with the problem-solving steps. "Remember— be a user of USAR. Understand, Strategize, Attack, and Reflect."

The problem of the day is: *A wizard has counted fourteen animal feet in his home. He only has were-wolves and bats. What are all the possible combinations of werewolves and bats the wizard might have?*

"What kind of loser only counts feet?" Devesh jokes. "That's the real problem. Count the heads, idiot."

The classroom buzzes as students start talking in groups.

"Just ask your parents," Devesh says, more interested in my tournament trouble than in work.

"My parents don't even know I play."

"So tell them. And tell them you're real good too."

"Are you crazy, dude?" Hugh says. "He can't just tell them he's been doing stuff he's not supposed to do. Not all parents are like yours."

"Everyone our age plays *Cross Ups*. It's not nearly as bloody as *Real War* or *Mega Haunt*."

I sigh. "You don't get it. Even Josh isn't allowed to play."

Devesh's monobrow shoots up. "What? But your brother's sixteen! He has his driver's license and his mommy won't let him play video games? That's messed up."

"You guys play together all the time," Hugh says.

"Not when our parents are around. Mom flips out at us when it comes to that stuff." I wag my finger at my friends and use my mom's Chinese accent. "Play violent game, lead to violent action."

Hugh and Devesh let out a burst of laughter, and Mr. Efram looks up from his desk.

"Why is your mom so against fighting?" Devesh says. "She comes from the land of kung fu. My parents are from the land of Gandhi and non-violence, but they couldn't care less about me going on a killing spree in a game."

"That's because your parents let you do whatever you want, dude." Hugh understands. His parents are divorced and he lives with his dad, who's kinda strict too. He's not so concerned about violence, but he does limit Hugh's screen time. Me and him are probably the only kids at Layton who don't have a cellphone.

"You want to trade and live at my house? Trust me, the Meanies would drive you crazy!" Devesh calls his three older sisters—Meenal, Shamini, and Minisha—"the Meanies," even though they mostly just spoil him like his parents do.

Hugh pushes his glasses back in place. "Uh, guys, Mr. E is still looking at us."

We work out all the possible combos to answer the problem of the day. I take notes with black marker on the big sheet of chart paper.

"Three werewolves and one bat," says Hugh.

"Two werewolves and three bats," says Devesh. "And one werewolf and five bats."

"Let's put zero werewolves and seven bats too, just in case he's trying to trick us."

"Good idea," Devesh says. "Mr. E loves that kind of thing."

While I write the reflection sentence that Mr. Efram always insists on, Hugh's attention is focused on something in the next row. He uses his math book as a cover and whispers, "Ty and Flash are doing it again."

I glance over. Ty, shielded behind his long blond hair, is obviously reading the answers from our paper to Flash. And just like a faithful sidekick, Flash is scribbling them down. The lightning streaks shaved into his tight black curls practically pulse with the effort.

"Just ignore them," I say.

"They always copy our work." Hugh turns his bulky frame to physically block the other boys' view.

"They're just lazy," Devesh says.

"But they do it every day now, dude."

"Then let's just do this." Devesh turns our paper over on the desk.

Ty yells, "Why you turning over your paper? You think we're copying you?"

"How'd you notice he turned over the paper so fast if you weren't looking at it in the first place?" Hugh calls back.

"What's going on here?" Mr. Efram walks over to us.

"Nothing." I give my friends a look that says drop it. "We're done, sir. Can we start on our homework now?"

I can almost feel a red dot on my forehead from Ty's laser glare.

Of course, we don't actually start our homework.

"I need to come up with a way to go to T3."

Hugh shakes his head. "Sorry, dude. We're smart but not that smart. If you can't convince your parents, it's not going to happen."

"Unless you lie about your age . . .," Devesh says.

CHAPTER 4

When I get home from school I hear the familiar sounds of a battle coming from the living room. The music is loud, and with all the grunts and explosions I know Josh didn't hear me come in. I loop through the kitchen so I can enter the living room from behind the couch.

I drop to the floor and crawl, military-style, toward the couch so I don't make any shadows that might give me away. The image from the TV screen reflects on the glass doors of the cabinet next to me.

Josh is playing his main, Cantu, the hydra-cross. In *Cross Ups*, all the characters start out as human fighters and turn into mythical creatures when they perform their Super moves. I watch and wait for him to play one of Cantu's Supers. When her neck divides into the multiple serpent heads of Hydra, I launch myself over the couch and tackle Josh to the ground, sending the controller flying through the air.

"Waaaaaaah! Holy crap, J, you idiot!"

"Scared ya!"

Josh stands up and tucks the green Chinese pendant he always wears back into his T-shirt. "Loser! You're lucky I didn't totally beat the crap out of you just now. I thought you were a home invader or something until I noticed how skinny you are. I could have thrown you across the room."

He's not exaggerating. Josh is almost double my size. I zoom back into the kitchen, partly to avoid being beat up and partly because I'm hungry.

Josh follows me. "You made me mess up that fight, nerd. Now Mario won and I'll never hear the end of it."

"Come on, stop playing with that loser. Play with me. Of course, then you'll have less chance of winning..." At the fridge I scan the selection of leftovers Mom brought home from her job at the diner and grab a container of noodles.

"Look, I'll play you," Josh says, grabbing the noodles out of my hand, "but show some respect. You're forgetting who taught you everything you know. Plus, if *I* don't play with you, who are you gonna play with?"

He's got a point.

"Okay, I'll go easy on you then. I'll even let you pick what character I play."

He's already back on the couch. "I don't need help to beat you, little brother . . ."

"Yeah, you do," Melanie calls from the front hall. She and Roy must have come in when Josh was screaming.

"Yeah, Jaden's the man. I can't even beat him if he plays with one hand," Roy adds.

"I know. I watched you try the other day. It was pathetic." Josh opens the selection screen. He picks Cantu for himself and Lerus, the unicorn-cross he knows I hate, for me.

For the hundredth time in an hour Lerus spears Cantu with her horn and stomps on her head.

This must be what Yuudai Sato feels like when he plays with his friends. I yawn. "Can I play Kaigo now? I need to practice a move." I really want to figure out how I hit the Dragon Fire Super yesterday.

Josh tosses his controller to the side. "Do whatever you want. I gotta go do some homework."

"Sure. That's what I'd say too if a guy four years younger than me was owning me." I stick out my tongue and make the "rock on" sign with my fingers.

"Well then, as your much older and wiser brother, I suggest you stop playing and do your homework too."

"If you're so much wiser than me, why can't you beat me anymore?"

"Oh please. That's hand-eye coordination, not intelligence. You play a lot, and your fine motor control is awesome. Too bad your gross motor skills suck. Later we can take it outside and shoot some hoops. I'll remind you who the real man is." He sticks out his tongue and makes the "rock on" sign back at me. "But seriously, Mom and Dad will be home soon. Turn the game off."

I stash the *Cross Ups IV* disk, with the plain blank label we placed over the original, in the case for the latest NBA game. Josh's number one rule when he started sharing his games was: never leave any evidence lying around.

I follow him up the stairs. "You ever think about entering a video game tournament?"

"You still making fun of me?"

"No, I mean for real."

"Nah. Why?"

"Just thinking it would be fun." I kind of want to tell Josh about Kn1ght_Rage and T3, but I know he'll make fun of me because I can't compete at real sports. He's always MVP and I've never even made a team. Even his part-time job is at a sports store.

Sadly, everyone in my family is sportier than me. Dad plays every sport and coaches some of Josh's teams. Melanie is on her school's golf team— although Josh says golf isn't a real sport. Even Mom still plays soccer in a league on Sundays. How pathetic is it that my mom is more athletic than I am?

"Well, don't bother asking Mom."

"Don't ask Mom what?" Melanie calls as we pass her room.

"Nothing," we answer in unison.

"Why is Mom so uptight about this stuff anyway? Cali says her mom calls our mom a 'real tough woman.' Why would anyone think Mom is tough?" I flop onto my bed so my head lands on my Kaigo pillow. When I look up, Melanie's standing in our bedroom doorway.

Even though they are twins, Melanie and Josh don't have anything in common besides the round, green pendants they always wear on red string around their necks. Even then, Josh always hides his inside his T-shirt while Melanie proudly displays her piece of Chinese culture. They definitely do not have that special "twin bond" people talk about.

They fight.

A lot.

I usually take Josh's side, partly because he's a guy and partly because we share a room.

As usual, Melanie joins our conversation without being invited. "Uncle Sammy said something like that

once too. About how he and Mom went through a lot back in Taiwan, but Mom told him not to talk about it in front of me."

"They had another brother." Josh swivels on his chair. "I think he died young or something. One time, there was a report on the news about some guy getting shot and killed, and Mom left the room, crying. Dad said it was too hard for her to watch because it reminded her of her brother."

"How'd he die?" I ask.

"Maybe he was a soldier in a war," Josh says.

"Duh, there was no war in Taiwan when Mom was a kid." Melanie rolls her eyes.

"I don't know." Josh shrugs. "I just know that whenever I used to bug her to let me watch a movie or play a game that she thought was too violent, she'd get this look on her face, like she had bad heartburn. Then she'd scrunch her lips together and take these deep breaths through her nose like an angry bull. After a while I just stopped asking."

"Yeah, I get the angry-bull look too." I sigh.

"I don't know why you guys want to play those stupid games anyway," Melanie says. "They're such a waste of time: living in a pretend world, as a pretend person, pretending to beat up other pretend people."

"Thanks, sis, you're right. We should spend more time walking across fields and rolling a ball into a hole like you, because golf's not a waste of time." He leans over and shuts the door in her face. Then he opens our laptop.

I stare at the stars on our ceiling that glow in the dark at night, my thoughts drifting back to the tournament. Man, it sucks that Josh is the one old enough to sign up for T3, but I'm the one with the skills to actually win.

CHAPTER 5

Mom is at the sink washing dishes. "Come on, *er zi*, eat your breakfast." As always, she speaks to me in Mandarin and calls me *er zi*, son.

"I'm not hungry." As always, I answer in English. It's not that I can't speak Mandarin, I just don't. English is easier. As I take my bowl to the sink, I feel a jab from Josh's student ID in my jeans pocket.

"What's the matter? You don't feel well?" She puts her hand on my forehead, and the jade bracelet she always wears for good luck slides up her arm, along with some sudsy water.

"I'm fine, Mom, just not hungry."

"What did you eat last night? Junk food? I know you kids don't eat well when we're not home."

"I'm fine, Mom. Really." I eat a spoonful of cereal from my bowl on the counter. "See? Fine. Don't worry so much."

We continue with the dishes in silence. People often say I look more like my mom than Melanie and Josh do. I worry that means I'm going to be short like her too. I notice my shoulder is now as high as hers. That's a good sign.

Dad comes into the kitchen with the day's paper in his hand and does a double take. "You feeling okay?"

"That's what I say." With Dad, Mom speaks English. She still has a Chinese accent. "He look sick to you?"

"No, honey. I'm just surprised to see him doing dishes, that's all."

None of us have Dad's blond hair and blue eyes. The twins both have light brown hair; mine is jet black. Josh's skin burns in the sun, but I end the summer tanned like crispy Peking duck. And where Melanie's eyes are round, mine are thin and definitely Chinese.

Dad tousles my hair and looks at me closely. "Actually, wait, he does look a little stressed. Jaden, I think there's something you need to give me."

My breath stops. Josh's ID burns against my leg. How does Dad know? I follow his gaze down to my hands and notice that my thumbs are tapping against my index fingers like they always do when I'm nervous. Dad raises his eyebrows. It takes me a second to notice he's holding up the cover of the sports section. "Montreal lost last night. They're officially out of the playoffs. So, hand it over, son."

I exhale. "Oh, yeah. I was hoping you wouldn't notice. I'll go get it." I run upstairs to grab the mini Stanley Cup that me, Josh, and Dad pass back and forth throughout the season, depending on whose favorite team is up in the standings.

Dad calls behind me, "And tell your brother to hurry up."

Josh is sitting on the floor of our room surrounded by a mess. He has dumped everything out of his backpack and now he's stuffing it all back in with much more force than necessary.

Should I give the ID back? But then he'll want to know why I took it. I'm in too deep. Might as well go for it now.

My stomach feels gross, and I wish I hadn't eaten any of that cereal. Without looking at Josh, I tiptoe through the mess and grab the toy trophy from the shelf over my bed where I keep all of my action figures. Josh has a shelf over his bed too, but his is full of actual trophies. Normally, he'd rub it in that I lost the prize, but this morning he doesn't even notice.

I run back downstairs, hand the cup to Dad, and grab my bag from the hook by the door. "I'm gonna take the bus today," I say.

"Don't be so upset, Jaden. We all knew this day would come." Dad kisses the cup like he just won the real thing.

I rush out the door faster than a Dragon Fire Super.

In math class I hold the ID next to my face. "You think I can pull it off?"

"Totally!" Devesh nods and goes back to placing the points on our graph for the problem of the day.

Hugh puts his glasses on and examines the photo. "I don't know, dude. I mean, you can pass for thirteen no problem, but this ID says you're sixteen." He picks up the ruler and starts connecting Devesh's points.

"You just have to go in acting confident. I'll come with you," Devesh says.

"And your brother is huge and looks way more white than you," Hugh continues.

"You worry too much," Devesh says. "No one's going to look that closely."

"You really think so?"

"And anyway, what's the worst thing that can happen?" Devesh asks.

"They could take away the ID card and call the police," Hugh says.

Devesh waves his hand at Hugh. "The registration is at a comic book store. They're not going to call the police over this."

"You sure?" I ask.

"Of course." Devesh sighs. "Don't you guys watch TV? The police don't have time to deal with fake IDs. The worst thing that can happen is the guy says you can't go to the tournament. So what? That's where you're at now, right?"

"That's true." I pause. "Okay, I'm gonna do it."

"Fine," Hugh says. "Now, what are we gonna do about Ty and Flash? Could they make it any more obvious? Ty is standing on his chair."

"Just let them look. Who cares?" Devesh rolls his eyes.

"No way. Why should we do all their work for them? We are *not* going to do that, are we, J?" Hugh's face is turning red and he's clenching his fists.

I think about it. "I don't know. Maybe Dev has a point. It's not like we'd be giving them some ground-breaking equation that we slaved over for months. These questions take us about twenty seconds to solve."

"Relax, Hughie. The sad thing is they copy our work but they still get it wrong," Devesh says. "Last week, when they copied our geometry, they must have read my writing wrong. Under 'proof,' they wrote, 'a triangle has *two* sides.'"

"That is kind of sad," Hugh says, his hands relaxing.

When the bell rings Mr. Efram calls out, "Will and Tyrell, I need to speak to you."

Ty shoots us a look and mouths the word *snitches*. Next to him, Flash pretends to use a knife to cut his throat open.

CHAPTER 6

"Do you think Mr. E figured out they're copying us?" Hugh whispers as we walk down the hall.

Devesh punches him in the arm. "Duh. You think he's keeping them in to tell them they're getting the math award this year?"

"Dude, why are you so mad? Isn't it good? Now they'll have to do their own work and stop using us," Hugh says.

Devesh glares at him.

"Not that simple," I say. "Did you see the death stares we just got? Now we have bigger problems than them copying us."

"But we never told on them. They can't be mad at us!"

Devesh stops. "Why don't you go tell them that, Hughie?"

Hugh puts up his hands. "Okay, never mind. Are we still going to the comic book store after school, or what?"

—◄o►—

It's raining when we step off the bus in front of the strip mall.

"What do I say?"

"Just say what he told you to say. 'Kn1ght_Rage sent me to sign up for T3.' Just be cool."

"Easy for you to say, Dev. I'm never cool. Can't you go in and sign up for me?"

Hugh shakes his head. "No way. You hardly look like your brother yourself. There's no way that Dev is going to pass as Josh."

We walk up to the door of Fly By Knight Comics. I reach out to grab the handle, then change my mind and spin around, crashing into Hugh's bulky frame.

"Ow. What're you doing, dude?"

"I've got to plan this better. I'm not ready."

Devesh grabs my shoulders and looks me in the eyes. "That's the beauty of it. When you plan out what you're going to say, you sound like a robot. Remember your speech about Pythagoras for math class?"

"Yeah, that sucked, dude," Hugh says.

"First off, put your hands in your pockets. When you tap your thumbs like that it's so obvious you're nervous."

I look down. Devesh is right; I'm tapping again. I stuff my hands in my jeans pockets.

"Now, just pretend you're Josh," he says. "What would he do? Be Joshua."

"Seriously?" Hugh waves his hands in front of him like a magician, laughing. "'Be Joshua.' That's your advice?"

I take a deep breath and let it out. I feel the student ID in my left pocket. "Be Joshua. That actually makes sense."

"Good. Let's go, before you change your mind." Devesh pushes me to the door and looks back over his shoulder at Hugh. "You stay out here."

Inside the store Devesh nudges me past the large bins of comic books straight to the counter.

"Can I help you boys?" A bearded man in his thirties wearing a *Star Trek* uniform shirt looks up from the comic on the counter in front of him.

Devesh pokes me in the ribs.

What comes out isn't much louder than a whisper. "I'm here to sign up for the Top Tiers Tournament."

"What?"

Devesh cuts in. "Kn1ght_Rage told him to come by and sign up for T3. Said he'd waive the fees."

The Trekkie looks me over. "Oh yeah? What's your gamertag, kid?"

"J-J-JStar . . . sir."

The Trekkie rifles through papers under the counter. "Yeah. You're on the list. You must be good if Kn1ght_Rage scouted you out. Here's the form." He pushes a piece of paper on a clipboard across the counter.

I fill in the lines with a pen attached by a string to the board. Then I hold it out shakily, but the Trekkie doesn't notice for a few more pages of his comic.

He skims the form and looks at me. "You need to bring your mom or dad in to sign the consent form. The tournament plays 13A games."

"He's sixteen. Show him your ID, Jo-shu-a." Devesh hits my hand, which has started tapping again. I shove both my hands back into my pockets. I pinch Josh's ID and start to slide it out.

The Trekkie eyes Devesh. "According to the birth-date here, he's not turning thirteen until December. Sorry, kid. Just get your parents to come in and sign the form."

OMG. Epic noob fail of the century. I shove my hands deeper into my pockets and turn to go.

"What . . . but . . ." Devesh stares at me, his mouth hanging open.

I head to the exit, but Devesh doesn't give up as easily. "Can he take the form home to his parents? They're really busy people and they don't have time—"

"Nice try, kid." The Trekkie snorts.

Defeated, Devesh follows me to the door.

Outside, Hugh rushes us, rain dripping down his glasses. "So, you in?"

CHAPTER 7

The rain has stopped, but my hair and clothes are drenched and my running shoes are slooshing when I walk down the street to my house. I don't even care.

The front path is covered with fallen cherry blossoms, their life cut short, just like my tournament dreams.

Cali is on her porch swing again. Her head is bent over a book and her long, black hair covers most of her face. My squeaky shoes on the steep porch steps make her look up.

"Looks like you had a crappy day."

I tell her the story.

"Ouch, that sucks."

"I don't want to think about it anymore. I'm gonna go in and beat some people up before my mom gets home."

"Uh, sorry to report, your mom's already home. She got here about ten minutes ago."

"Nothing's going right today." I'm glad Cali's here, at least. I've missed hanging out with her. "You never told me what was the matter yesterday."

"Oh . . ."

My door opens and Mom steps onto the porch. "*Er zi*, why are you standing here soaking wet? Come inside." She notices Cali. "Xin Yi, why are you sitting outside?" Cali is my only friend that Mom can speak Mandarin with. She calls her by her Chinese name, *Xin Yi*. "It's raining. Come in. Do you want to eat dinner with us? I'm making your favorite, *mapo* tofu."

"*Xie xie, A Yi*." Cali thanks her. Unlike me, Cali always speaks Mandarin with our moms.

"You sit on the porch a lot lately. Is everything okay with your mom?"

"She's sleeping. I didn't want to wake her."

"She's not well again?"

"It's been pretty bad lately."

In Mandarin, Cali sounds like a different person. When I look closely, she looks different too. There are dark circles under her eyes.

Her mom's always had this disease that makes her clumsy sometimes so she trips and drops things. But most of the time she's okay. I can't remember what it's called. When I open my mouth to ask about it, no words come out.

Mom says, "Eat with us and bring her home some food too. *Lai, lai.* It's too wet outside."

Dinner feels like old times. Cali and I always used to eat at each other's houses. Now that I think about it, I can't remember the last time I saw Mrs. Chen. Was it before Christmas?

When everyone's done eating, the stories start. "Remember when your mom was Jaden's piano teacher?" Melanie says.

"What?" Cali shakes her head.

"Yeah, it didn't last long. He was a lost cause," Josh says.

Just like everything else I tried. Except gaming.

"Every time Jaden was supposed to have a lesson, he said he had a stomachache to get out of it," Melanie continues, playing with her green pendant.

Dad joins in. "So I took him to the doctor. She

wanted to do an x-ray and run tests. Jaden got scared and fessed up that his stomach was fine, he just hated piano."

I really don't think Cali wants to hear stories about someone pretending to be sick when her mom is actually sick. "So, is everybody done?" I get up and start taking dishes to the sink.

"Wow! This morning you did dishes, now you're clearing the table." Dad points to Mom. "See, Linda, I told you he'd come in handy one day."

"He just doesn't want us to keep telling embarrassing stories in front of Cali," Melanie sing-songs.

Mom joins me in clearing the table. "You must eat here more often, Xin Yi. My kids use better manners when you are around."

Cali gives a weak smile. "*Xie xie, A Yi*. Dinner was delicious. I'm going to take this to my mom now." She holds up the leftovers Mom packed up for her.

"Tell your mama I will visit her tomorrow," Mom says.

I want to say something too, but I can't figure out what before Cali heads out the door.

—◅○▻—

After dinner, I sit at the desk in my room staring at my homework but thinking about Cali. How did I not realize that her mom was so sick? I can't believe I went on and on to her about a video game tournament.

Josh comes into the room and starts packing up his baseball gear for practice. "I think it's time you get your own gamertag. I keep getting these annoying messages from your friends when I'm playing."

"No way. I'm the one who built JStar up in the standings. You get a new gamertag."

"I don't think so. I had it first. Anyway, who the heck are Catchup and GodofGods?"

I smile at Hugh and Devesh's onscreen names.

"Or Kn1ght_Rage?"

I pretend to be really busy with my homework.

"He wrote a weird message saying he heard from a friend that I'm only twelve years old."

I don't look up. "Oh, yeah. I played that guy the other day. What'd you say?"

"I ignored him. Hey listen, don't go talking to strangers online, okay?"

"Yeah, I know."

"No, seriously. That could be anyone, like some creepy old perv. I heard about this one kid on the news. He went to meet some online friend to trade hockey cards and it turned out to be this old guy who wanted to take pictures of him—*naked*." Josh gives a shiver of disgust, then stops to pick something up off the desk. "Hey, how'd my ID get here?"

"Oh, that? I found it under my bed just now. Must have fallen down there." I keep my eyes on my paper.

"Aw man, I looked everywhere for this thing." He shoves the card into his pocket, grabs his bag, and flies out the door.

—◄○►—

The next morning before school, Ty and Flash march across puddles toward us. Ty calls, "So, which one of you told Mr. E that we copied?"

"We didn't say anything," Hugh counters.

"Probably all three of them told." Flash's voice is much louder than it needs to be.

"You guys think you're sooo smart." Ty moves right up in my face. "We're not stupid. We know you ratted us out to Mr. E."

"I told you, we didn't say anything," Hugh fires back, fists clenched. "We didn't need to. You guys are so obvious. Do you think Mr. E is blind?"

Devesh grabs Hugh's shoulders and pulls him back. "Just drop it, Hugh."

"These guys are total snitches." Ty plays it up to the crowd that has gathered.

The bell rings like it's the end of a round in a boxing match. Me and Devesh immediately grab Hugh's sleeves and pull him like a prisoner of war to the main doors.

In the distance, Ty continues to rant to anyone who will listen.

Hugh struggles out of our grip. Punching the locker in front of him, he says, "But we didn't say anything. What the heck is their problem?"

"It's not worth it," I say.

At lunch the three of us sit by ourselves in the cafeteria, trying to act like we don't see Flash and Ty pointing at us.

On our way to my place after school, Hugh sums it up. "They're telling everyone who will listen their side of the story. And people believe them."

"I know," I say. "Everyone was giving me the evil eye in the halls. In geography, Ryan coughed into his hand, and I'm sure he said, 'Snitch.'"

"I can't believe they're making this into such a big deal," Hugh whines.

"Who cares? By next week everyone will forget their stupid lies."

"I hope you're right, Dev. If the rest of the year is going to be like this, I don't know what I'll do." I'm serious too. I work hard to blend into the background at school. I can't handle all those people staring and talking about me.

"I want to blow some things up. Let's play *Blast 'Em Up* today instead of *Cross Ups*," Hugh says.

"Yeah, I might as well stop playing *Cross Ups*. It's too depressing. I just keep thinking about the tournament."

Devesh stops a few doors down from my place, smiling wider than his monobrow. "Yo, things are looking up. There's a hot girl on your porch."

"What?" I look over. "That's just Cali."

"*That's* your friend Cali?" Devesh looks from me to Cali and back again, jaw wide open.

Hugh sighs. "I guess she doesn't want to play *Blast 'Em Up*, huh?"

"She might. We used to play together a lot. She's pretty good."

Devesh and Hugh answer together. "Awesome!"

CHAPTER 8

"Holy crap, she's good," Hugh loud-whispers to Devesh.

It's a couple of hours later, and they're slouched on the couch with a laptop between them. Me and Cali are sitting cross-legged on the floor, controllers in hand. We were all losing to Cali until I challenged her to play *Cross Ups*.

"Don't tell anyone a girl beat us all at *Blast 'Em Up*," Hugh says.

"No? I was totally just going to send it out to everyone, loser." Devesh is live-streaming the game. "Check this out. I've got eight viewers."

"You think she can beat J at *Cross Ups*?"

"Nah, but she's coming closer than we ever do. Did you see that? She just turbo boosted her Super Meter with that move."

"How'd she do that?" Hugh grabs Devesh's arm. "No way! She's throwing Saki's Blizzard Super."

Saki is the yeti-cross so, obviously, this Super move causes a snowstorm to bury his opponent. Like Kaigo's Dragon Fire Super, the Yeti Blizzard Super is really hard to time.

My block comes fast enough, so I take minimal damage. I throw a series of fireball combos to run Saki's Health Meter down to critical level. One last hit is all I need to win.

It doesn't feel right though. I turn to Cali. "Call it a tie?"

I can feel Hugh and Devesh freaking out behind me. Hugh loud-whispers, "What?"

"Thanks. Won't your mom be home soon anyway?" Cali asks.

"Nah. She works till nine tonight."

"Well, I should get back to my mom." She turns to Hugh and Devesh with a shy smile. "Nice meeting you guys. Sorry for hogging the controls."

"No prob. We, uh . . . we can play a lot better, you know. It's just this thing at school . . .," Hugh stammers.

Devesh elbows him in the ribs and smiles at Cali. "What he means is, 'Nice to meet you too.'"

Cali gets up, and I follow her to the door.

"I don't remember you being that good at *Cross Ups*."

"Well, I've been staying home and gaming a lot since my mom's been sick." She bends down to get her running shoes.

I want to ask about her mom, but what should I say? "How . . ." I swallow and glance back at the living room where my friends are craning their necks to stare at us. "How, uh . . . how're you at *Death Raid*? We should play. Just come over whenever." Oh, that was weak.

"Yeah, maybe. Thanks." She slips out the door carrying her shoes in her hands.

When I get back to the living room, a message is blinking on the screen. Devesh and Hugh, still staring down the hallway, haven't noticed.

Kn1ght_Rage   Friday, 6:45 pm
Y D1DN'T U F1N1SH H1M?

"What should I say?" I ask.

Devesh follows my eyes to the screen, but Hugh, still staring at the front door, says, "A pretty girl who can play like that? I say, ask her to marry you."

"What?" I say.

Devesh grabs Hugh's head and turns it to look at the television. "He means Kn1ght_Rage, moron."

"Oh."

Devesh picks up the controller and taps in

JStar   Friday, 6:46 pm
SAVING IT 4 T3

I punch Devesh in the arm. "Uh, that would be great if I was going to be there."

Kn1ght_Rage   Friday, 6:47 pm
U C0M1NG T0 T3?

I reach for the controller, but Devesh jumps over the back of the couch with it. Before I can stop him, he types *YES*.

"What the . . . ?" I tackle him and wrestle the controller from his hands. "Why'd you put that?"

"Because you have to go." Devesh moves quickly backward to avoid my punch.

Kn1ght_Rage   Friday, 6:48 pm
GR8. S33 U TH3R3

Kn1ght_Rage signs off.

"You're an idiot." I throw the controller at Devesh.

"Relax, we'll figure something out." He climbs back over the couch and sits down. "But first I want to know the same thing that Kn1ght_Rage does. What was that? You've never pulled a punch for either of us before."

"Yeah. You never offered to call it"—Hugh flutters his eyelashes—"a tie."

I shrug, but I can feel Kaigo's dragon breath on my cheeks. "It's not like that. She's just got a lot going on right now, so I cut her a break."

CHAPTER 9

The next morning I hear the school bell, but I don't want to go in. I think of Ty and Flash and their stupid comments and consider skipping the day. Then I notice that the bell sounds different. Instead of the usual brisk, metallic ring, this bell sounds more like a rhythmic whine, and it doesn't stop.

I wake up and jump out of bed to look out the window. It's Saturday, and that sound isn't a school bell, it's an ambulance. I throw on jeans and a T-shirt and run downstairs.

I pull open the heavy front door. Through the screen I can see Cali on the porch, half hidden behind the bulky frame of a police officer. I hear the words *MS* and *interferon*, whatever that is.

I notice another sound and look down to see my hands against the door. As usual, my thumbs are tapping, wishing for a controller. That's not helping. I need to get out of hit stun and do something.

I push the screen door open and walk out. There isn't enough space on the porch for me to get around the officer, so I'm stuck behind him. Two paramedics come out of Cali's house, carrying Mrs. Chen on a stretcher. As they pass Cali says "I love you" in Mandarin.

Mrs. Chen's skin is pale, somehow thinner. She holds her arms strangely in front of her chest, wrists bent like she's about to play the piano. I realize that I haven't heard her play in months.

"We're going to help your mom, honey," the police officer says. "Is there someone you can stay with? Who can we call for you?"

Cali stares down at the ground. Her tears drip like rain on the porch boards.

"She can stay with us," I say, but my voice is lost in the slam of the ambulance doors.

"Or, we can take you down to the station . . ."

"I guess I could call my da—"

Mom bursts out the door in her bathrobe, a towel wrapped around her hair. The officer moves aside, almost tripping over me. Mom puts her arms around

Cali and hugs her tight to her chest. "Don't worry," she says to Cali in Mandarin. Then she turns to the officer. "Which hospital?"

—◦—

Mom and Cali don't get back from the hospital until late. Dad takes care of dinner.

While I can't figure out what to say to Cali, Dad goes into funny-guy mode. He holds open the pizza box, and in a tough-guy voice says, "Hey, you want a pizza me?"

"Don't smile," Melanie warns, "it only encourages him."

"Do you know how to fix a broken pizza?" he asks.

Cali shakes her head.

"With tomato paste, of course."

"No, don't laugh," Melanie insists, "or else he'll keep going."

"Don't worry, I won't tell any more pizza jokes. They're all too cheesy."

We all groan, including Cali.

After dinner, Dad sets up an extra mattress in Melanie's room for Cali.

I hang back in the kitchen with Mom. "How's Mrs. Chen?"

"*Hao*." Good. She smiles and continues. "They are taking good care of her. Her disease is very bad lately. She's been having trouble with her muscles. This morning she fell on the stairs because of it and broke her leg. She's lucky she didn't hit her head."

She finishes her slice and goes to the sink to rinse her plate.

Dad walks back into the kitchen and Mom switches to English. "Cali need a good friend now. She is a tough kid. Been through many problems already even so very young."

"Sounds like someone else I know." Dad winks at Mom.

◄○►

The next morning after breakfast, Cali and me are the last ones at the table. Dad and Melanie are at a golf tournament, and Mom drove Josh to his job at Sportworld. We stare at our empty plates.

Cali breaks the silence. "Wanna play *Cross Ups*?"

"My mom will be home any minute."

"We could go to my house."

"Never thought of that. Aren't you going back to the hospital today?"

"Your mom said she'll take me after lunch. Gaming helps me not think about all that stuff. We can play something else if *Cross Ups* makes you think about the tournament."

"Whatever. It doesn't matter that much. It's not like . . ." I want to say "life or death," but that's stupid. You don't talk about death to someone whose mom is in the hospital.

"I know you wanted to go, but I didn't think you'd actually lie to enter."

"I tried, but I'm not a good liar."

"I think deep down you didn't want to go against your mom and that's why you messed up."

"Maybe. Or I was too nervous."

"Well, I think you're just a nice mama's boy." She winks. "If you want to prove me wrong, don't pull any punches today. Let's go."

CHAPTER 10

When the school bell rings on Monday morning, I stand behind the play structure at the end of the field and watch everyone enter. Who am I kidding? I'd never skip school. Cali's right, I am just a mama's boy. I wait a few more minutes, then finally go in.

At my locker, I find the word *Snitch* carved into the metal. Nice. Just what I need.

I don't see Devesh and Hugh until math class, just before lunch.

"Guess who's going to T3?" Devesh announces when I come into the room.

"Who?" I sit down next to my friends, who are smiling like they just beat me at *Cross Ups*.

"You, dude. You're signed up." Hugh holds up his hand for a high five, but I leave him hanging.

"What did you do?" I ask Devesh through clenched teeth.

"I told you I'd think of something. Yesterday I asked my dad to take me down to the store. I got him to sign the form first. Then, instead of my information, I put yours. There was some other guy working behind the counter. I just told him I was JStar and he waived the fee. It was so easy."

I stare at Devesh.

"Uh, you're welcome. Here's the schedule and the official rules." He hands me two sheets of paper.

"You owe Dev big time, dude." When I don't say anything, Hugh adds, "I think he's still in shock."

I stare at those papers. I think about how Cali called me a mama's boy. It's true—part of me was relieved when the lie at the comic store didn't work. I don't like the idea of going behind my mom's back.

But I have another side—my Kaigo side. And he's showing Mama's Boy who's boss.

Kaigo reminds Mama's Boy how awesome it felt to beat Kn1ght_Rage.

Jab to the head.

He tells him it will be even more awesome to beat Kn1ght_Rage in person.

Uppercut.

He says I can't let my friends down.

Flying sidekick.

Plus, I already play *Cross Ups* behind mom's back, what's one more lie?

Sucker punch.

This battle in my head drowns out everything around me for the entire math class. When the bell rings, I get up to go.

"Where are you going, dude?" Hugh asks. "We have to stay, remember?"

I look around at the rest of the class filing out the door, talking and laughing. Then I notice Ty and Flash sitting at their desks too.

When all the other students are gone, Mr. Efram closes the classroom door and positions himself between our two groups.

"Gentlemen . . ." He leans on a desk and rests his hands on his stomach. "It doesn't take a genius to see that there is some tension between you." He looks at each of us sternly. "Any comments?"

I look at my desk. My mind screams at Hugh to keep his mouth shut.

After a pause long enough to upgrade my gaming system, Mr. Efram pulls out last week's assignment.

"You see, boys, as I was showing Tyrell and Will last week, your two assignments are almost identical." He points from one paper to the other. "Except that this one says 'a cube has six faces' while the other says 'a cub has six feces.'"

Flash and Ty look at each other blankly.

Next to me, Devesh's body shakes. Hugh's lips press together tightly to keep from smiling. Fortunately, I'm not in the mood to laugh.

Mr. Efram continues. "It seems clear to me that there is some copying going on. There is also some obvious discord between you all. So, what are we going to do about it?"

Silence.

"Okay, if you don't have any ideas, I have one."
More silence.

"I can tell you are all eager to hear it." He smirks.
"Since you three"—he circles his right hand to indicate me, Devesh, and Hugh—"find this class easy,
I'm going to give you a challenge. You will tutor
Will and Tyrell here." He tips his hand to indicate
the other boys.

A loud groan from Hugh and a collective
"Nooooo" from Flash and Ty break the silence.

"Listen. I'm sure once you guys get to know each
other better, you'll find that you have more in common than you thought. And by working on math,
you'll be productive at the same time. Your first session is tomorrow after school. I'll meet the five of
you here." Mr. Efram gets up and walks to the door.
"Don't be late."

CHAPTER 11

BAM! I smash open the front door and drop my bag on the way down the hall. The controller is in my hand within seconds.

I find some noob online and start smashing him up. Man, I want to go to T3 so badly now. At least then there would be one good thing in my life. Why should I feel guilty about going? It wasn't me who lied to sign up; it was Devesh.

Kaigo's going ham on the screen. He smashes his opponent's head into the ground over and over. *Crack! Crack! Crack!* I'm starting to feel a bit better.

Click, click . . . that sound did not come from the game. What is my mom doing home so early? I bolt into shutdown mode. Where's the remote? I throw the couch cushions up in a panic. Then I spy it at the other end of the couch and lunge. Too late.

"*Er zi!* What are you doing?"

I'm sprawled on my stomach like Superman, the fingers of my right hand just inches from the remote. I keep my head down.

"Why are you playing this? I said no fighting."

I don't move. With my face squished into the couch cushions, I can hardly breathe.

I hear Mom's purse clatter on the ground and feel her sit down by my feet. "*Er zi*, you are not supposed to play games like this."

The need for oxygen makes me pick up my head. Even though there's no point, I grab the remote and stare at it. It's vibrating like a volcano about to erupt because my fingers are tapping it so fast.

"This game is so violent."

"It's not so bad, Mom." My voice is barely more than a whisper.

"Not so bad? That guy was hitting the other guy's head on the ground. Blood was spraying everywhere!"

I bite my lip and take a deep breath in through my nose. My mother is doing the same. It's the angry bull.

On screen, Kaigo is getting his butt kicked.

"You know, if you do that in real life, someone will die."

The remote explodes out of my hands, and with it come the words. "I wouldn't do that in real life, Mom! It's just a game! Why do you have to make such a big deal out of it?" I walk over and jab the power button on the TV.

The room is silent. I have never yelled at my mother before. I turn to her with my head down and look at her from under my eyebrows.

She looks like I just sucker punched her. I look away.

Her response comes after a long pause. "See how you act to your mother? You think it has no effect on you to beat up people like that? You don't know what violence can do to people. Do you want to turn out like my brother?"

I wonder if she is crying, but I can't bring myself to look at her again.

"Go to your room."

◄o►

It's after midnight and I'm staring at the fake stars on my ceiling because I can't sleep. When I got to my room this afternoon I was so mad I punched the wall. Hard. The knuckles of my right hand still ache. Sad part is, I didn't even put a dent in the wall.

I can't stop thinking about what Mom said. Maybe beating people up on the screen *is* making me more violent. Why else would I take a swing at the wall?

And what the heck did my uncle do? Am I really like him?

My stomach growls. I didn't eat much dinner because I wanted to get away from Mom as fast as possible. I roll out of bed and head downstairs.

The light is on in the kitchen and my eyes are still adjusting when I hear, "Hey."

Cali's sitting at the table with a glass of milk. Her pink pajamas are covered with silver hearts and her knees are pulled up to her chest.

"What're you doing up?" I ask.

"Couldn't sleep."

"I guess a mattress on the floor isn't so comfortable."

"No, it's fine. I just couldn't stop thinking."

I sputter, "Oh... yeah." I'm such a loser. Obviously Cali has bigger problems than I do. I pour myself a glass of milk, add several squirts of chocolate syrup, and stir, all using my left hand.

"My mom taught me this game to help me relax and fall asleep. You think of a topic, like 'boy names,' and then you go through the alphabet and say one that starts with each letter. Like Andrew, Bill, Carlos ... It always works, and I fall asleep before the letter Z. But tonight I did it with movies, TV shows, songs ... I think I went through the alphabet at least ten times. I finally gave up and came down here."

"Wow, that sucks."

"I miss my mom." Her voice is a whisper.

"Isn't she coming home soon?"

"The nurse said maybe on the weekend."

"So that's good, right?"

"I guess. It's just . . . I miss having her around. She's the one I talk to about all my problems . . ."

I sit down across from her. I want to say, *You can talk to me,* but that sounds weird, like something someone would say in a movie.

We sip our milk in silence. Cali's reflection in the dark window looks older, like her adult self is sitting next to her.

"So I hear you got grounded."

"Melanie?"

"Actually, I overheard your parents talking about it."

"Yeah, my mom flipped. Then I flipped. It was bad." I walk over to the cupboard for some cookies. "What'd they say?"

"Your mom was pretty mad. Your dad said it's normal for boys to play those kinds of games. Why does everyone always say that? Girls play too."

I bring the bag to the table, open it, and awkwardly pull out three cookies with my left hand. "Dad stuck up for me? Cool." I shove a cookie in my mouth and then remember my manners. "Wam sum?" I point to the bag.

She takes one and nibbles. "Sorry. It's kind of my fault your mom got home so early. She changed her work schedule so she could drop me at the hospital. Sounds like you're going to be under surveillance 24/7."

I swallow. "Pretty much. I have to go straight to my mom's diner after school for the next month. She did make an exception for math tutoring. So, basically, no freedom at all."

"At least I know where to find you." Cali dunks her cookie into the milk.

"Except for *maybe* Saturday." I should shut up, but I don't. "I haven't decided for sure, but I might be telling my parents I have to do extra math tutoring."

"Okay . . . why?" She tilts her head and looks at me while dunking the rest of her cookie.

"Devesh got me signed up. I'm still trying to work up the guts to go."

"Hmm. Interesting . . ."

A light goes on upstairs, and Mom's voice calls in a loud whisper, "*Er zi*? Are you down there? Go back to bed. You have school tomorrow."

I wish I knew how Cali was going to finish that

sentence. Does she think I should go to the tournament or not? But the moment is gone. "Better go," I whisper. "Don't want to deal with the angry bull again." I stuff one last cookie in my mouth and head upstairs.

CHAPTER 12

The next day after school, me, Devesh, and Hugh hesitate at the door to Mr. Efram's classroom.

"Come in, boys," Mr. Efram calls from behind his desk. "Your friends aren't here yet."

"Friends?" Hugh mouths, raising his eyebrows.

We sit down at our usual desks. Devesh puts his head down and closes his eyes.

I *so* do not want to be here. I'm tired. My hand hurts. I can't take being around Ty and Flash right now.

After a while Hugh asks, "If they don't show up, can we go?"

"I'm sure they'll be here any minute, Hugh," Mr. Efram says.

As if on cue, Ty and Flash slink through the door.

The teacher gets up and motions for them to sit

down in the seats in front of us. Then he pulls up a chair next to me.

"Great! We're all here. I'd like you to start by taking a minute to think of something the other group doesn't know about you."

Devesh whines, "Mr. E, what does this have to do with math?"

"Why can't we just do our homework and go home?" Ty says.

"This activity will help you get to know each other better. It's important for you guys to feel connected in order to work well together. So, who wants to go first?"

The room goes silent, like someone pressed mute.

"Okay, it was my idea, so I'll get the ball rolling. One thing you probably don't know about me is that I have a huge comic book collection." Mr. Efram turns and looks at me expectantly.

Why me? I shrug and try to act casual. Maybe he'll skip me.

No luck. He's not backing off. But I can't formulate a single sentence that answers his question. It's like the comic store all over again.

He nudges my elbow with his. "Come on, Jaden. The faster you all play along, the faster we'll get to the math part."

The other boys are staring at me. I need to say something to make them stop. I open my mouth and what spills out is, "Uhhh . . . I'm going to be in a video game tournament on Saturday."

"Alright. See? I bet Tyrell and Will didn't know about that. Now, Will, what can you tell us about yourself?"

"I have a dog," Flash answers.

We continue around the group and discover that Devesh is wearing blue underwear, Hugh likes ketchup on everything, and Ty also has a dog.

"Okay, that was great, boys!" Mr. Efram's voice is full of fake enthusiasm. "Now let's take a look at tonight's homework, shall we?"

We all pull out our books. After checking that everyone knows the assigned question numbers, Mr. Efram goes back to his desk.

For the next half hour, we sound like an after-school special called *How to Help Your Friends with Their Homework.*

Hugh: Let's use the problem-solving steps.

Devesh: Remember to be a user of USAR.

Me: Step 1: Does everyone *understand* the question?

Hugh: Step 2: Let's *strategize* and make a plan.

Devesh: Step 3: Time to *attack* the question.

Me: Step 4: Don't forget to *reflect* on the answer.

Every once in a while, Mr. Efram calls from across the room with instructions like, "Make sure you don't give them the answer, Hugh," or, "What does Tyrell think is the next step?"

When all the assigned questions are answered, we pack up and quietly exit the classroom.

"See you tomorrow. Same bat-time, same bat-place," Mr. Efram calls after us with a chuckle.

The five of us walk in silence. At the bottom of the stairwell, Ty and Flash block our path.

"Don't show up tomorrow," Ty says.

Devesh raises his monobrow. "Are you telling us what to do?"

"I'm telling you what *not* to do. It's easy. Don't be there." Ty crosses his arms.

Flash runs his hands across the lightning streaks over his ears. "Just don't come, okay? We've got a volleyball game after school tomorrow, but Mr. E says we have to be at tutoring. But if you guys aren't there, there's no tutoring and we can play."

"We're not taking orders from you," Hugh says.

"It's important, okay?" Flash whines. "Three guys on the team got chicken pox. If we don't show, there won't be enough players and the team has to forfeit."

"Uh-uh." I shake my head. "Talk to Coach Lee or something. If we don't show up, we're going to be the ones in trouble."

"Coach sided with Mr. E," Flash moans.

"These guys don't get it. They've never even played on a team." Ty clenches his fists and bangs them together. His bright blue eyes stare at me. Then he turns them back to Flash. "Did you hear? Our pal Jaden is going to be in a video game tournament. What are you playing, Jaden? Virtual sports? Or do you even suck at those?"

"I bet he's playing Pokémon."

"Shut up," Devesh says. "Why don't you guys go home and play with your dogs."

"He's not playing P-P-Pokémon." Hugh's glasses slide down his nose. "He's playing *Cross Ups IV*, and he could beat you up any day." His voice rises to a squeak on the word *day*.

"Oh, he can beat me up any day?" Ty mocks Hugh's high-pitched tone.

I stare at Hugh.

"I mean in *Cross Ups*," Hugh mumbles.

"What losers." Flash laughs.

Ty laughs too. "I know, right? *I can beat you up in my video game*," he sings.

"Whatever." I push past Flash. "I'm going home."

Ty grabs my sleeve.

"Let go of me, jerk."

Ty pulls me right up to his face—so close I can smell the tuna sandwich he had for lunch. "Or what? You gonna beat me up with your superpowers?"

I bet my uncle wouldn't have let idiots like Flash and Ty push him around. He was probably more like Kaigo. I wish this was *Cross Ups* and I could go super-combo crazy on these guys right now.

The pain in my knuckles reminds me of my pathetic punch yesterday. Reality check: if I tried to throw a punch I'd probably whiff.

Devesh pushes me hard to get me out of Ty's grip. Then he puts his arm behind my back and steers me out the school doors. Hugh runs after us.

"If you guys show up tomorrow, we'll beat you so bad you won't be able to play video games for a month." Ty and Flash stand at the doors, chests puffed out, heads held high.

CHAPTER 13

I get to the diner around five o'clock and go straight to a booth in the back corner. The smell of the vinegar I love to pour over fries mixed with the grilling burgers from the kitchen makes my mouth water.

I pull my math book out of my backpack and flip it open to the place where I shoved the tournament papers from Devesh. Even though I've already memorized the information, I unfold the pages and stare at them.

A few minutes later, Roy comes over and sits across from me in the booth. He's been waiting tables at the diner to earn money for college ever since he finished high school last year. Even though Mom says she doubts Roy will ever actually go to college, I know she appreciates his ability to keep even the crankiest customer happy. Still, Melanie hasn't gotten up the nerve yet to tell our parents she's dating Roy.

"You haven't been here in a while." Roy slaps me on the shoulder with a dish towel. "What's up?"

"I'm grounded."

"No way. What'd you do?"

"Got caught playing *Cross Ups*."

"Man, your mom is so strict. I guess she's the same at home as she is here. At least she's not making you work in the kitchen as punishment, eh?"

"She wants me to focus on school." I point to the math book on the table.

Roy looks around, then drops his voice. "Okay, but whatcha really doing?"

I look down at the book.

Roy flips it open to the T3 sheets. "Ohhh, no way. You little rebel." He covers his mouth and looks around again. "How're you going to get there if you're under watch?"

"I'm not sure I'm going yet."

"But if you were going?"

I look across the diner. Mom's taking an order by the windows. I whisper, "I could tell my parents I have to tutor these guys from school for a big math test. If I leave at ten, catch the 38 East bus, then transfer to the 78 North, I'd get to the tournament by ten forty-five. The *Cross Ups* competition is from eleven to one, so I should be back by one forty-five. Only problem is, if I make top eight, I need to stay longer."

"Wow, good luck."

"I told you, I'm not sure I'm going."

"Listen to yourself. There are flash mobs that happen with less planning than that. You're going."

Roy has a point. My plan is pretty awesome. "Hey, don't say anything to Mel, okay? I don't need her ratting me out."

"My lips are sealed." Roy closes the textbook and heads back to the kitchen.

At lunch the next day, I find Devesh and Hugh in the cafeteria. I pull out my lunch—leftover meatloaf from the diner. Like always, there's a sticky note on top of the Tupperware container with Chinese writing. I crumple it up and shove it in my jeans pocket before the guys notice.

Hugh rips open three ketchup packets at once and squirts it over everything on his tray. Then he shovels a forkful of red goop into his mouth.

"How the heck do you eat that crap?" Devesh asks.

"Better than your stinky fish curry," Hugh answers, still chewing.

Devesh takes a forkful of fish and waves it in front of Hugh's nose. Then he moans, "Mmmmm," and slurps it off his fork.

"You guys are both gross. So, what's the plan for after school today?"

"Let's recap," Hugh says. "Option one: we go to tutoring and Ty and Flash beat the crap out of us. Option two: we skip tutoring and Mr. E calls our parents."

"They're not going to beat us up, Hughie. There are two of them and three of us," Devesh says.

Hugh rolls his eyes. "Doesn't mean they won't try."

"If we don't show up, they're going to think they own us," Devesh says.

I shake my head. "How is it that two guys who totally suck at problem solving came up with this plan?"

We all sigh.

I say, "What if we ask Mr. E? If we act like we

care about Ty and Flash maybe he'll be so happy we're getting along that he'll change his mind."

"Maybe." Hugh doesn't sound convinced. "But what if he says no? I think it's better if we don't go and just say we forgot."

"Yeah, we'll say we didn't hear him when he said, 'Same bat-time, same bat-place.'" I mock Mr. Efram's voice.

"Okay, so we'll bolt when the bell rings and meet at the bus stop," Hugh says.

"And then what? We just do whatever Ty and Flash tell us to from now on?" Devesh says.

"Just this one time. I can't take anyone else being mad at me today," I say.

"Fine." Devesh grumbles. "What's the plan for Saturday? Want my dad to pick you up?"

"Yeah, thanks, dude." Hugh smiles.

"I mean Jaden, moron. He's the one competing, and he actually lives near me."

"I don't know," I say. "What if your dad talks to my parents?"

"Hmm. Never thought of that. My dad does like to chat. So how're you getting there?"

"Probably take the bus."

"But you'll still come pick me up, right?" Hugh asks. "What time will you be at my place?"

My last class is French. Halfway through class I pack up my things and sit at the edge of my seat. At the bell I explode toward the door.

Madame Frechette blocks the way. "*Où vas-tu?*"

"*Pardon?*" I ask in my best French accent.

"*C'est à ton tour de lever les chaises, Monsieur Stiles.*"

"*Pardon?*" I look around wildly for a clue to what she might mean.

"Put up the chairs," a classmate whispers on her way out the door.

I run around the class and place each chair on a desk at lightning speed. Then I call, "*Au revoir,*" over my shoulder and scramble down the hall. Just as I turn the last corner, I smack into something huge and fall backward onto the floor.

I look up.

Mr. Efram is staring down at me. "Wow! You are one enthusiastic tutor. I'm not even at the classroom yet and here you are racing to help your peers. Now that is dedication." He offers me a hand.

I'm in hit stun. "I . . . uh . . ." The next thing I know, I'm climbing the stairs next to my teacher in the direction of the dreaded math class.

"Today I thought you guys could review the problem-solving steps again. I think that would be very helpful for Will and Tyrell."

"But, I, um . . ." My mind races, but I can't come up with any logical reason not to follow Mr. Efram to class.

It's a warm day, and the upper floor feels a lot warmer than downstairs. At the end of the hall Flash and Ty lean against the wall outside the math classroom wearing their volleyball uniforms and kneepads. When they spot me next to Mr. Efram, Ty straightens up and clenches his fists. Flash sinks to the ground, eyes closed in defeat.

I slow my pace, falling behind Mr. Efram.

The teacher enters the classroom, but Ty and Flash wait for me. When I get to the door, Ty leans in close and whispers, "You are so dead."

CHAPTER 14

The next forty minutes are a blur. Words like *understand*, *strategize*, *attack*, and *reflect* tumble out of my mouth, but most of what I say makes no sense because my mind is focused on all the ways Ty and Flash could hurt me. I imagine Flash ripping actual lightning bolts out of his hair and throwing them at me.

My hand isn't hurting much anymore, so I spend most of the time writing with my head down. Ty and Flash are silent, but they kick me hard under the table whenever Mr. Efram's back is turned. At one point, Ty draws a hangman and labels it "J-din." That's one I hadn't thought of.

Finally, Mr. Efram walks over and asks if Ty and Flash understand the steps.

They lie.

"Alright, boys. Let's call it a day."

Ty and Flash bolt out of the room, leaving half their stuff on the desks.

I pack my bag super-slow. It's warm in here. Is that why I feel like I can hardly breathe? When Mr. Efram turns off the fan by his desk, I take the hint and stand up. I look around wildly for some excuse to stay in this room. "Mr. E, can I . . . help you clean the boards?"

"No, thanks. It's too warm in this room. I'd like to head home. Oh, and Jaden, tell your friends they'd better have a good excuse for not being here. I don't take this kind of behavior lightly."

"Yes, sir. I'm sure they have a good reason."

"Mmhmm."

I stop at the doorway, watching Mr. Efram pack up his briefcase.

"Is there something you want to say, Jaden?"

They're going to kill me now. I swallow. "No, sir." I head out of the classroom.

I'm pretty sure Ty and Flash turned right and took the usual route to the main entrance. I turn left and duck into the boys' bathroom. Maybe if I stay here long enough they'll give up waiting for me and go home. I lock myself in the last stall and lean against the wall. It takes me a second to realize the tapping sound I hear is coming from my own thumbs. Too bad there's no cheat I can input to get me out of this situation.

The bathroom door opens slowly. Through the crack in the stall door I can just make out two forms coming in. I quietly climb up onto the toilet seat and hold my breath, but I'm sure they can hear the sound of my pounding heart.

"Jaden?" a voice whispers.

"It's us." I recognize Hugh's voice, despite the whisper.

I exhale, climb down from the toilet, and open the stall door with shaky hands.

"What the hell happened?" Devesh asks.

As quickly as possible, I tell them the story.

"We knew something was wrong when you didn't show." Hugh whispers like he's on a spy mission. "We came back to look and saw you in Mr. E's class, so we waited around the corner."

"Did they go home?" I ask.

Just then, the bathroom door bangs open, answering my question.

"Well, well, look who's here: the traitor and his

little friends." Ty crosses the room in two giant steps. "We missed our game because of you, loser." Ty is up in my face.

"No, you missed your game because you're failing math, loser." Devesh pushes Ty away from me.

"Oh, so you want to fight?" Ty looks at Devesh.

"Let's see what video game moves these guys have," Flash says.

"Wait, guys, listen, you don't understand." I talk as fast as my thumbs tap. "I wasn't going to come today. Mr. E saw me on the way out of school and forced me." I put my arms up like I'm surrendering and start to maneuver myself around Ty and Flash. "Sorry you missed your game. We're leaving." My back is to the door now, and I start to back toward it.

"I don't think so." Ty follows me. "We missed our game and now you're gonna pay." He raises his arm to throw a punch, but Hugh's scream distracts him. Devesh grabs Ty from behind, pinning his arms to his side.

When he sees what Devesh has done to Ty, Hugh tries to grab Flash in the same hold. Flash pushes him off with ease and lunges at Hugh. With another scream, Hugh runs toward a stall, stumbles, and lands on the floor. Flash trips over Hugh, goes head first into the stall, and thunks his head against the toilet.

Hugh scrambles to his feet and pulls the door shut. "I got him," he yells, both arms outstretched, pulling the stall door closed.

I refocus on the target in front of me.

"Hit him, J." Devesh is fighting to keep hold of his struggling captive.

He was going to do it to me. Why not? A million possible moves from *Cross Ups* run through my head.

"Think of all the times they copied off us," Hugh calls.

"Yeah, and all the dissing, man. Just hit him." Devesh's grip loosens as Ty writhes in his arms.

All of the week's frustrations pour into my head. I pull back my arm. Then my mom's words flash into my head. *Do you want to turn out like my brother?*

I drop my fist. "I'm not gonna fight."

"Well, that's good news." The voice comes from behind me. I turn to see Mr. Efram at the door. "What's going on in here?"

—◁◦▷—

It's almost six o'clock by the time I get to the diner. Mom rushes over even though there's a line of customers waiting for tables.

"*Er zi*, where have you been?"

"Tutoring ran late and there was a bit of a problem." Mr. Efram said he's going to call all our parents. I'm not sure how much to tell her.

"What kind of problem?" She's whispering now, which is kind of silly since I don't think any of the customers speak Mandarin.

"Some of the guys wanted to get in a fight . . ." The beginnings of the angry bull begin to cross Mom's face. "But nothing happened. Don't worry."

"Go do your homework. I'll talk to you in a minute." She breathes in deeply through her nostrils and goes to seat the next customers with a fake smile.

I slump into my usual booth near the kitchen. Almost immediately, Roy appears. "Your teacher just called and asked for your mom. I took a message since the place is swamped. You need me to lose that message?"

I smile. "Thanks, man."

"No problem. How goes the crazy bus plan for getting to the tournament? You know I could give you a ride over, eh? I'm not working this weekend."

"Thanks, but I've got it covered. Remember, Mel can't know anything about this."

"I get it. You want to take care of everything yourself. It's time for you to spread your wings and fly. You're growing up so fast." He pretends to sob into his dish towel as he heads off to pick up meals from the kitchen.

A few minutes later, Mom's shadow looms over my science book. This time I'm really doing homework.

"*Er zi*, what do you mean there was a fight?"

"No fight. It was just a big . . . misunderstanding. The teacher sorted it out. That's why I was late getting here."

"I don't like to hear you are involved with this kind of thing. Maybe I should tell your teacher you can't do tutoring anymore."

Actually, Mr. Efram decided to cancel the tutoring sessions until he talks to all of our parents. Mom doesn't need to know that. I feel my alibi slipping away and quickly reply. "No, Mom, it's okay. Actually, we're moving tutoring to Saturday mornings now. So I can come straight here after school every day."

"The school is open on Saturday?"

"Uh, yeah. Mr. Efram is coming in to supervise us."

"He's a very dedicated teacher." She pauses. "Fine. But if there are any more problems, I will call your teacher and say you can't do this anymore."

She believes me, so why don't I feel happy? All I feel is an ache in the pit of my stomach.

CHAPTER 15

Cali's face is red and blotchy when we pick her up in front of the hospital.

"What happened, Xin Yi?" my mom asks.

"The nurse told my mom"—she takes a wobbly breath—"that she'll need a wheelchair for at least a few months. That means she can't come home . . . she wouldn't even be able to get up the front steps." Cali inhales. "So my mom called my dad and"—she sobs out the last words—"I have to move in with him."

Wow! I totally forgot that Cali even has a dad. Her parents have been split up for as long as I can remember.

"But you'll stay with us during the week for school, right?" I ask.

She shakes her head, squeezing her lips together to control the tears. "It's too far. I have to transfer to a school in . . . in . . . Montreal."

Now I remember Cali going to Montreal a couple of times to see him. But that's so far.

"I'll talk to your mom. Maybe I can convince her to let you keep living with us." She sounds confident, but her thumbs are tapping the steering wheel like mine do when I'm nervous. Is that an inherited thing?

"*Xie xie, A Yi*, but I'm pretty sure her mind is made up. My dad is driving down on the weekend to get me."

"Why can't you just get a wheelchair ramp?" I ask.

She sighs. "That's what I said. Then the nurse told us it costs, like, two thousand dollars. Mom hasn't been working lately, so we can't afford that."

When we get home, me and Cali climb the steep porch steps and sit on her swing, facing each other, knees bent. The toes of our running shoes overlap in the middle.

I try to imagine life without Cali. My whole life she's always been right next door.

"Remember Spy Club?" she asks.

I look down through the floorboards. I can just make out the old kid-sized table and chairs we picked out of the trash one day and excitedly installed in

our clubhouse under the porch. From this secret spot we used to spy on the neighborhood.

We swing in silence for a while.

Cali's voice is shaky when she talks again. "I can't believe these six steps are ruining my life."

◄o►

When I get to my room, Josh swivels the desk chair around to face me. "Okay, what do you have going on with this Kn1ght_Rage guy, bro? He keeps sending spam about the Top Tiers Tournament like you're going to be there. Today it said, 'Biggest prize pot ever.'"

I cough. "He probably just wants more people to sign up. I think he messages everyone like that."

"Are you sure? Who is this guy, anyway? He uses all these numbers instead of letters. Who does that anymore?"

Good question. "Don't know. I only talked to him that one time when I beat him." I'm not lying.

"What? You beat him? That guy is godlike. He's got the highest score for four different games. I looked him up."

"Yeah, so?" I flop on my bed and grab my MP3 player from under the Kaigo pillow.

"Obviously it's *you* he wants to see at the tournament. Next year you should totally go. If you win the whole thing, that's two grand. Crap! Now *I* wish you could go!"

I stop short of putting my earbuds in place. "Two thousand dollars? Is that what he said?"

"Yup. It would take me five months to earn that kind of money from my shifts at Sportworld."

Sweet! I was so excited to compete, I hadn't even thought about prize money.

◄○►

"Mr. E called my house," Hugh says the next morning in the schoolyard. It's already warm out, and the curls on his forehead are damp. "My dad was waiting for me at the door. Funny thing was, he just wanted to know if I was alright."

"That's weird. You didn't get punished?" I ask.

"No. I couldn't believe it either. He was all, 'Buddy, you should've told me you were having trouble with kids at school.' Not sure what he thinks he would have done to help."

"Lucky you." Devesh shakes his head. "I *am* grounded. No T3. Man, I've never been grounded before. What the heck am I gonna do all weekend?"

"If your parents don't take away your computer, you can watch the live-stream," Hugh says.

"I guess. But I totally want to be there. What about you, Jaden? What happened?"

"I got lucky and Roy 'lost' Mr. E's message." I make little finger quotes next to my head.

"That's cool." Devesh punches me in the shoulder.

"What do you think happened when he called Ty and Flash's places?" Hugh asks.

"Good question."

We spend the morning looking over our shoulders

for them. By the time we get to math, it's clear we can stop looking.

"You think they're skipping?" Devesh asks.

"Maybe they got suspended."

"We could ask Mr. E . . .," I start. "Actually, I'm gonna stay off his radar today."

By the afternoon the heat makes the second floor of Layton unbearable. Most teachers have the classroom windows open wide, but in Mr. Efram's class, that's not an option. The room only has two high windows. One is boarded up where a foul ball broke the glass earlier in the year, and the other window's handle is rusted shut. Mr. Efram is melted into his desk chair, the class's only fan directed straight at him. Instead of concentrating on the problem of the day, we spend the period doing our own math— calculating ways to spend two thousand bucks.

"You could buy, like, every game out there," Devesh says.

"Who cares about games, dude, you could get a whole new system and probably your own computer too." Hugh's arms wave wildly around his head.

"Oh, and make sure you get a phone." Devesh puts his hand on my shoulder. "It's about time."

Hugh nods.

"Maybe I'll buy an air conditioner for this room."

"Or . . ." Hugh's eyes go wide. "You could get a monkey. That would be awesome."

I laugh. "What am I supposed to do with a monkey? Anyway, I might not even get there, let alone win." Besides, I've already decided what I'll buy if I win the tournament.

At the end of class Mr. Efram stops me at the door. "Your mom never returned my call yesterday."

"Oh, you called?" is all I can think to say.

"Yes, I told you I would. I left a message with someone at your mom's work. I guess I'll try your dad at lunch."

"Okay," I mumble and slink out the door.

When I get to the diner after school, I know Mr. Efram got through. It's only 3:45, but Dad is sitting in a booth by the window in his suit and tie. He's never finished work this early, so I must be in serious trouble. Mom's sitting across from him spinning her bracelet. Her name tag is on the table.

At the back of the diner, Roy peeks through the

kitchen opening at me, wringing a dishcloth like a nervous old lady.

I walk over to my parents, ready to receive the touch of death. As usual, Mom does all the talking, but in English because Dad's here.

"Your teacher called."

"I told you yesterday. Nothing happened."

She looks so small sitting in the big booth across from Dad. Then she lets out an angry-bull breath and I wish I could back dash right out of the diner. "He said there is no more tutoring. Why you say you have tutoring Saturday?"

Oh crap. "I . . . um . . . thought there was still?"

"Well, we find out soon. I told your teacher we meet him today."

CHAPTER 16

Five minutes later I slide across the hot leather seats in the back of our car, earbuds in place even though the batteries in my MP3 player are dead. I really don't want the lecture.

Dad drives while Mom fidgets with her bracelet. She's turning it back and forth so fast it's like she's trying to force good luck out of the thing.

At a traffic light, Dad puts his hand on hers. "Let's just go and hear what the teacher has to say."

"Sorry. I can't help thinking of Li Yun."

Li Yun. Is that her brother who died?

A few minutes later, we all walk silently into the school. Mr. Efram ushers us into an empty, air-conditioned conference room. "Have a seat."

"Thank you for meeting with us, sir," Mom says as everyone sits down around the table.

"No problem, but you really didn't have to come down here. I only called to make sure you were aware of the incident that took place yesterday. Did Jaden tell you what happened?"

"He only say there was a fight but nothing happen. How can a fight be nothing? It sound like something to me." Mom takes a deep breath, and Dad puts his hand on hers again.

"What my wife is trying to say is that Jaden is a twelve-year-old boy, so we only got the bare bones of the story." He chuckles.

"Well, let me fill you in then." Mr. Efram explains what he saw in the boys' bathroom. Just like Hugh's dad, he finishes with, "I only wish Jaden had told me earlier about the problems he was having with these other boys. Perhaps I could have intervened before things got ugly."

"So, Jaden was not fighting?" Mom asks.

"On the contrary, he was the peacekeeper."

"Oh, that is good. I was so worried. You know, he play terrible video game and I think maybe he get idea . . ."

"Yes. Jaden told us he entered the Top Tiers Tournament this weekend. That's exciting."

A tapping sound starts up. It takes me a second to realize it's my thumbs.

"What tournament?" Mom looks back and forth between my teacher and me. "Is that why you lied about tutoring Saturday?"

I look down and try to control my thumbs.

Mr. Efram clears his throat. "Uh-oh. Have I opened a can of worms here?"

"Seems so." Dad leans forward.

After a long pause, Mom speaks. "Jaden is not allowed playing those games. I catch him playing a fighting game and now he is grounded."

"Oh . . . I see." Mr. Efram looks at Dad.

My thumbs are out of my control.

"My wife is quite worried that violence in video games can lead to violent behavior."

"Well, I would have to say, based on yesterday's incident, that doesn't seem to be the case with your son."

I peek up.

Mr. Efram gives me a wink. "I've done a lot of research into how boys learn, and video game violence comes up quite a bit in the literature. It seems there has to be a predisposition toward violence in order for there to be any real effect from playing the games. Jaden is clearly not a violent kid, otherwise he would have taken a swing at those bullies yesterday."

Is Mr. Efram actually defending me?

"Mr. Efram makes a good point, Linda," Dad says.

"To be honest, I think a video game tournament would be a great experience for Jaden. You know, he doesn't participate in any extra-curricular activities here at school. It would be good for him to get out there and compete at something he likes."

What? Did he actually just say they should let me go?

"This is not basketball or soccer," Mom says. "In these games he beat up others and"—her voice drops to a whisper—"sometimes I think he kill them."

I jam my lips together to squash a smile.

"I'm sure he does," Mr. Efram says. "That's kind of the point of the game. But Jaden's smart enough to make the distinction between reality and fiction. It's not Jaden performing those actions, it's a character he's playing. Heck, I play video games. I don't have a violent bone in my body, ma'am, but I sure do love to beat up an ogre on screen. I don't think you need to worry about Jaden. He's a good kid. That said, you are the parents and you must decide what you think is best for him." Mr. Efram gets up.

My parents do the same. They shake his hand, and we head out of the school.

CHAPTER 17

That meeting with Mr. Efram was a total cross up. Who would have expected a teacher to tell my parents I *should* play video games? It's like we've entered another dimension. Even the drive home feels different; for once, it's Dad who does the talking.

"So, what's this competition your teacher was talking about?" he asks as we pull out of the parking lot.

"It's just this tournament where people compete at this game."

"What game is that?"

I pause. What difference does it make anymore? "It's called *Cross Ups IV*."

"Uh-huh." Dad looks at Mom. She's staring out the window, calmly turning the green bracelet on her wrist. She doesn't seem to be listening. "So, how do you play *Cross Ups IV*? What's the goal?"

"You just try to win battles."

"And how do you do that?"

"You have to know all the different combos."

"Combos, eh?" We're at a red light now. Dad turns around to look at me. "So, how often do you win these battles?"

"Most of the time."

"Really?" He raises his eyebrows. "How'd you get so good?"

I shrug and look down at my MP3 player.

"Never mind." Dad shakes his head and turns frontward again. "Stupid question." The light turns green. "So tell me, son, why'd you sign up for this tournament when you know you're not allowed to go?"

"I dunno. This guy challenged me."

Dad glances at Mom again and we drive along in silence for a while. Just as I'm about to put my earbuds back in, Dad asks, "How does all this relate to the problem with these boys from your math class?"

"It doesn't. Those guys just hate us for some reason."

Dad is quiet for a bit. Then he says, "You've obviously got a lot going on with these guys from school bugging you and Cali leaving. Just let us know how we can help you."

Might as well try. "You could let me go to the tournament."

Dad chuckles. "Well played. But I don't think your mom's gonna go for that."

We both look at Mom again. Still no angry bull. She's just looking out the car window, like she's staring into another world.

Dad pulls up in front of the diner. After Mom gets out and closes her door, I give it one last try. "Mr. Efram's a teacher and he thinks I should go."

Dad turns again to face me. "I know. But your mom feels very strongly about protecting you from this stuff."

"I'm not a little kid. I don't need to be protected."

"Just give her some time. I think she's starting to see that."

If only I had time. The tournament is in two days.

"That's cool that your teacher said you should go."

The air conditioner's not on at Cali's place, so it's pretty toasty up in her room. We're sitting leaning against her blue bedroom wall. A fan points straight at us, fluttering the edge of her blue bedsheet. We've been here for half an hour, but the suitcase on the bed is still empty.

"I never saw it coming. If only my mom agreed. It would have been amazing."

"Still no sign that she's going to let you go?"

"Nah. She's still mad at me. Anyway, whenever I talk to her lately, it's like she doesn't understand me. And it's not just because I'm speaking English."

"That's because you've been lying. You probably didn't make any sense because you were trying to keep track of what you said so you wouldn't get caught."

I wish Cali wasn't right.

She goes on. "At least now the lie is out in the open. You can start fresh."

Like it's that easy. "In case you haven't noticed, I'm not so good at saying the right thing. I'll probably just make it worse."

"There's only one thing to say."

I stare at her, blankly.

"Apologize."

I don't want to talk about this anymore. "Don't you think you should start putting some stuff in there?" I point to the suitcase.

"Yeah . . . No . . . I don't know." She drops her head to her chest. "Maybe I'll just pack tomorrow. I don't know what to bring. It's too hot to think."

We sit awhile in silence. Cali's room doesn't look like you'd expect a girl's room to look. There are no pink butterflies or flowers. Everything is blue except the white furniture.

There's a photo of Cali and her mom on the dresser. They're wearing red Chinese dresses and smiles wider than the happy Buddha in the background. With their faces pressed together, it's only the proud look in Mrs. Chen's eyes that shows she's Cali's mother and not her sister. That's how I picture Cali's mom—not the person they took out of here on a stretcher.

There's a poster of Captain Marvel and one of Hermione from Harry Potter, but I don't see any pictures of Mr. Chen in the room. "It feels like your dad's been in Montreal forever. When's the last time you saw him?"

"Last summer, for a week. At Christmas he sends a present. Last year he got me that bear." She points to a worn stuffed animal by her pillow.

"Man, that's gonna be weird, going to live with him—even weirder than living with us."

"It's not weird living with you guys. It's like my second home."

"Yeah, but rooming with Melanie . . ."

"She's nice, J. She's been doing stuff like braiding my hair and lending me clothes. Your whole family is nice. Your mom changed her work schedule a bunch of times to take me to the hospital. She's been treating me like I'm one of her kids. She makes my lunch and even puts little notes inside in Chinese. I'm not sure exactly what they say, but today I recognized the character *ai*, for love. Your place feels more like a home than I've had in a while."

I think of the embarrassing notes I toss out of my lunch every day.

We sit staring into space. A drop of sweat runs down my back and I break the silence. "You know the best thing about my place?"

"What?"

"It has air conditioning . . ."

◄◦►

The next morning when I get to my locker, Devesh sing-songs, "They're ba-ack."

I sigh as I twist the dial to open my lock. "So, were they suspended?"

"They're not saying," Hugh says. "But I'm pretty sure. Listen, we wanted to warn you. I don't think you're going to like this . . ."

I turn to look at my friends. "I'm not going to like what?"

Hugh tries to get Devesh to meet his wide-eyed stare, but Devesh puts his hand to his chin and looks away.

This can't be good. "What?"

Hugh gives up and starts rambling. "Well, I guess this doesn't count as bullying in the school rules. In fact, Mr. E might even think they're trying to be nice—"

"What are you talking about?" My voice must be loud because some kids in the hall turn to look at us.

The captain of the basketball team, who has never said a word to me before, walks by and gives me a double thumbs-up. "Rip 'em up, JStar."

"This is the worst warning ever. I have no idea what you guys are trying to tell me. Wait . . ." I whip my head around to follow the popular boy's path. "Did Holden just call me JStar?"

Devesh presses his lips together and inhales deeply through his nose. Without making eye contact, he puts his arm on my shoulder and turns me around. Hanging from the banister of the second-floor railing is a white bedsheet painted to look like a banner. My name is printed in huge letters, along with an invitation to watch me play at T3.

"What the . . . No . . . Oh, come on!" I imagine the entire school watching me compete.

"I know." Hugh puts his hand on my other shoulder. "Someone must have helped them. I mean, it's way too neat and there are no mistakes—even the website address is right."

Just my luck.

Suddenly, there's a lot of hype around me. Kids I've never talked to start coming up to me in the halls. They ask questions like, "What character do you play?" and, "What's your best combo?" There are a surprising number of gamers at Layton and they're all rooting for me, which would be great if I was actually going to the tournament.

Not everyone is so supportive. I turn a corner and hear, "Have fun fighting the big, scary monsters tomorrow. I hope the boogeyman doesn't get you," or, "So, you think you're a star, JStar?" These guys are going to be brutal when they find out I can't compete because my mom won't let me play the game.

I'd rather take a real live infinite attack than face these guys on Monday morning. I wish I could move to Montreal with Cali.

CHAPTER 18

Bam! Bam! Bam!

We enter Mr. Efram's room to the sound of him pounding on the rusty window latch. He can just reach the latch by balancing on a pile of math texts on a chair. It's another sweltering day, and the math class feels like the inside of one of Kaigo's fireballs. Mr. Efram's light blue shirt is blotchy with dark patches down the back.

"Wow, he's dripping," Devesh whispers as we take our seats.

Hugh mops his forehead. "This is the hottest room in the school."

I point with my chin toward Flash. He's deflated on his desk, head resting on folded arms. Above the lightning bolt on the left side of his head is a huge bulge that looks like a rain cloud. "Looks like

Hughie's the only one who left a mark the other day in the bathroom."

"That was the toilet bowl, not Hughie," Devesh says.

Ty struts over to me. "You like our banner, JStar?"

"Whatever."

Bam! Bam! Mr. Efram is totally punishing the rusty handle. "Come on, just open already!"

Ty says, "Now the whole school is going to watch you play. No pressure."

"So the whole school can see how good he is," Hugh snaps.

"Or watch him choke." Ty puts his hands to his neck and makes a gagging noise.

"Nah, he's way better than your volleyball team," Devesh says.

Before Ty can think of a comeback there's another *Bam!* from the window, followed by a loud, "Son of a . . . Borg."

The class snickers.

Mr. Efram steps down from the chair, shaking his left hand and wincing. "Well, it took all my superpowers, but at least I got that blasted window open." He tries to laugh, but what comes out sounds pained.

"In light of the temperature in this room, and the fact that I probably can't write on the board now, today I think we will focus on the last problem-solving step." Mr. Efram notices Ty standing by my desk.

"Tyrell, remind us what that is."

"Uh . . ." Ty looks at me. After a long pause, I roll my eyes and point to the poster on the wall.

"The last step is . . . uh . . . reflect?"

"Indeed." Mr. Efram walks back to his desk, collapses into his chair in front of the fan, and starts massaging his left thumb with his right one. "Take this period to reflect on a question of your choice."

I fall into my usual booth at the back of the diner and drop my head on the cool ceramic table. It's Friday. No point working on homework. I've got all weekend for that.

There's a light tap on my head, and I look up to see Roy grinning down at me. "What's the matter, kid? Thought you'd be all excited about tomorrow."

"It's not happening. I got found out."

Roy sits down across from me, and I quietly tell him about the meeting with Mr. Efram.

"So, the teacher said you should compete and your mom still said you can't go?"

"Well, she didn't exactly *say* I can't go, but obviously . . ."

"What did she say, exactly?"

I think for a bit. "Actually, we haven't talked since the meeting with Mr. E. I guess she's not talking to me, or I'm not talking to her, or whatever."

The cook rings the bell for an order pick-up.

"Man, if I were you I'd be all over her today, begging for a chance to go. You've got an endorsement from a teacher, bro. That's gotta count for something. You really want this, right?"

"Yeah, but . . ."

"You gotta fight for what you want in life, like you fight in your game. You'd never give up this easy in a battle." Roy heads for the kitchen.

Ten minutes later, Mom walks by. She puts a bowl of ice cream on the table as she passes. I take a deep breath and call after her, "Mom?"

She turns and walks back to me.

I hesitate. I look down and see my thumbs tapping. To stop them, I slide them under my legs. Cali's advice from the night before rings in my ears. Man, this is harder than Kaigo's Super. *"Dui bu chi."*

Her eyes widen. I don't know if she is more surprised that I apologized or that I spoke in Mandarin.

Strangely, it feels easier than saying sorry in English, so I continue in Mandarin. "I wasn't trying to be bad. It's just that everyone I know plays these games. And I'm really good at them." I pause to check for signs of angry bull, then continue. "I'm not a little kid anymore."

"I know you are growing up, but you are not that old yet."

"C'mon, Mom, even my teacher said there's nothing wrong with gaming. Studies show gaming actually helps kids with concentration and reasoning, which is great for problem solving in math." I read that online last night.

She sighs. "This game is very violent, *er zi.*"

"I have to go to the tournament. The prize is two thousand dollars."

"Why does a twelve-year-old need so much money?"

"If I win, I'm going to give the money to Cali's family for a wheelchair ramp. That way, Mrs. Chen can come home and Cali won't have to move to Montreal."

Mom bites her lip. "You are a good friend."

I catch a glimpse of Roy over Mom's shoulder. His dish towel is draped around his neck and he's hopping from side to side, shadow boxing.

It's now or never. "Please can I go to the tournament?"

Mom cringes. "I don't think that is a good environment for you."

Roy shakes his head and mimes an uppercut.

I can only think of one last possible move. I hope I'm not going to regret this. "What if you come with me? That way you can see what it's like."

Mom scrunches her eyebrows and mouth. Not angry bull, more like thinking bull.

"If you don't like it, we'll leave. I promise. I just want a chance to try."

After a long pause, she gives a tiny nod. "That's a fair plan."

I smile, and Roy raises his arms in victory, then quickly drops them when Mom gets up from the booth.

Aaah! I'm actually going to T3!

Wait . . . Aaah! I haven't played all week!

CHAPTER 19

That evening, I want to play *Cross Ups* and practice the Super that defeated Kn1ght_Rage, but my parents are home. Even though Mom agreed to let me go to the tournament, she didn't say I could play the game whenever I want. I don't want to push my luck by asking.

I turn on the laptop and scan the *Cross Ups* forums for tips on playing against Blaze. I want to figure out why I kept taking damage in that match against Kn1ght_Rage. One comment says that Blaze's Solar Burst Super has to be blocked from a crouch in certain situations. No wonder Kaigo kept taking the punishment! Too bad there are no tips to help me pull off Kaigo's Dragon Fire Super.

I think about watching some of Yuudai Sato's old matches for inspiration, but I don't think Mom will like that.

I head to Melanie's room to make fun of the music she's playing. She's painting Cali's nails, so I decide to hold on to my insult for next time.

"Having a little sister beats having brothers." Melanie is focused on Cali's hand. "You know, I've tried to do Jaden's nails a million times, but he always runs away."

"Ever try when he was sleeping?" Cali smiles at me.

Melanie looks up. "Good idea. Wanna help me tonight? Wouldn't he look great with hot-pink nails for his big tournament?"

"Ha, ha. I'll go now. I didn't mean to interrupt while you were practicing your future profession."

"Actually, we're done." Melanie closes the bottle of midnight-blue polish. "So, Mom and Dad are going with you tomorrow. Good luck with that." She gets up, places the bottle on her dresser, and starts brushing her hair.

Cali waves her hands around and blows on her nails. "That's cool they're coming to watch."

Melanie snickers.

"Mom only agreed to let me go if she can come along to check things out. Now it's both of them. Man, I hope Dad doesn't do anything lame."

"Your dad's not lame."

Melanie snorts. Just then, headlights from the street flash three times through the window. "That's Roy. See ya." Melanie waves out the window, grabs a lipstick, and rushes off.

"Don't you remember last year's school play?" I ask Cali. "I had one line, and after I said it, my dad stood up and clapped."

"Oh yeah. That was cute."

"Cute? Try embarrassing. Then this year I tried out for football and my dad came to watch. Turns out I suck at football. I get out from the very bottom of a huge pileup and my dad yells, 'You'll get 'em next time, son.' The grade eights laughed their butts off. Kept saying, 'You can do it, son,' and crap like that."

Cali doesn't laugh like I thought she would. "At least your dad comes to your stuff. Mine has never been to any of my things."

Ugh. I'm such a scrub.

Cali's dad is coming tonight, so she's finally taking the packing seriously. Too seriously.

"Can you help me get this thing closed?" Cali

presses on the top of the suitcase, but the two sides are still very far apart.

It's cooling off outside, and I sit by the window catching the breeze. "Not gonna happen. That thing looks like a python trying to swallow an elephant."

"But I need it all." She grabs my arm and tugs me to my feet. "Please. If we both push, it'll close."

"There's no way . . ." I notice her eyes are glistening. "Unless we sit on it."

I help her climb on top of the teetering pile, and the lid sinks down a bit. Then I step up on the bed and place one knee next to hers. The top drops some more. Slowly, like a circus performer climbing onto the top of a pyramid, I bring my other knee up beside the first. The lid goes down to within an inch of the bottom.

"We need to wiggle it down," Cali says.

"I don't—"

Before I get my sentence out, Cali starts bopping up and down. Not ready for the action, I slide forward. Cali grabs me, and the next thing I know we're both lying on the floor.

"You okay?" Cali's tears are tears of laughter now.

"Yeah. Sorry."

"It's okay. It was my stupid idea to bounce."

I start giggling. "You should have seen the look on your face just before we fell."

"You should have seen the look on yours!"

"Why don't you just get a second suitcase?"

She stops laughing. "I don't want to go."

"If I win tomorrow and use the money to buy your mom a wheelchair ramp, do you think they'll let you stay?"

"Aww, you're so sweet."

Sweet? What does that mean? I know what Hugh

and Devesh would say. I look into Cali's eyes, wondering if maybe my friends are onto something.

She gets up and rummages through her closet. She finds a duffel bag and starts throwing the overflow clothing into it.

I get up and stand next to her. "We'll email."

"Yeah." She sniffs.

I start to reach for some clothes, then think better of it. What if I accidentally grab her underwear or something? I say, "And we can play online."

"Uh-huh."

"And talk on the phone."

She stops and turns to me. She looks like she's going to crumple. Instinctively, I hug her. She smells good—like vanilla ice cream. What do I say? I think about what my mom would say and go with that. "It's going to be okay. You'll be back before you know it."

The doorbell rings. I let go.

Cali wipes her eyes, and I follow her down the stairs in silence. She sighs and pulls the big door open.

A Chinese couple stands on the porch. I recognize the short, skinny man as Cali's father, but not the roundish woman next to him. The woman's lips are pressed together, and her head bobs from side to side like she is silently humming along to music.

"Cali, open up."

Cali unlocks the screen door. The short, hefty woman grabs the handle and pulls it open, stepping on my foot as she pushes past us. Cali's dad calls after her, "It's down the hall on the left."

Her father steps in and gives Cali a one-armed hug and a pat on the head. "So, you all packed?"

Cali looks down the hall where the woman disappeared. "Who is that?"

"That is Marnie." Cali's father smiles a smile that makes his cheekbones stick out. There's a long pause, and for a second I wonder if he is going to say anything else. "She, uh . . . hmm . . . well, I guess you'd say she's my girlfriend." His cheekbones stick out more. "Sounds strange, though, when you're my age."

Cali stares at her father, mouth open.

"I thought it would be nice to bring her along so you two can get to know each other a bit on the way back to Montreal. Kind of like a road trip. That way, you'll feel more comfortable when we all get home."

I watch Cali's eyebrows disappear under her bangs. "All?" she asks.

The toilet flushes.

Her father clears his throat. "Marnie and I have been sharing a house for about a month now. You're going to like it. It's a lot bigger than my old apartment."

The bathroom door opens, and Marnie walks, much slower this time, back to join us in the crowded entryway.

"You must be Cali." The woman gives Cali a hug that is not returned. "And you? Richard only told me about one child to pick up." She launches into fake laughter.

"I'm Jaden. I live next door."

"Oooh, the boy next door," she sings. "Many a good romance novel starts with the boy next door." She double winks at Cali's father.

My cheeks get hot.

Cali's father holds up his keys. "I'll go and get our things."

Marnie says, "Once we're settled, we're going to take you out for a fancy dinner to celebrate." She gives a tiny clap.

"Celebrate what?" Cali asks.

"Why, celebrate you moving in with us, of course. I'm so excited! I don't have any children of my own—yet."

Cali stares at me, her eyebrows still lost somewhere high up on her forehead. Is this woman for real?

Mr. Chen struggles to get a suitcase up the steep front steps. I hold the screen door open for him.

Cali blinks rapidly as her father trudges past her. He's halfway up the stairs before she finally speaks up. "Where are you taking that?"

He rests the case on a step. "We're going to use the master bedroom, since it's empty."

"Yeah, nice of Mom to make space for you." Cali brushes past me out the door I'm still holding.

"Don't be too long. Our reservations are in an hour," Marnie calls after her.

CHAPTER 20

The next morning, I wake up before my alarm.

It's tournament day!

I shower, dress, and head down to the kitchen to join Mom at the breakfast table. Dad took Josh to baseball practice, and Melanie's still sleeping. It's both strange and comforting to be alone with Mom. I crunch my cereal while she drinks tea, her green bracelet sliding up her wrist whenever she takes a sip. I wonder what she was like when she was my age in Taiwan. What happened with her brother back then? It must have been bad if she's still freaked out about it now.

There's a knock at the door. Mom answers it.

I hear a man's muffled voice, then she calls to me, "*Er zi*, have you seen Cali this morning?"

"No." I go to the door.

Cali's father peers into our house. "She was gone when we got up this morning. Can you believe she left without saying anything? Didn't her mother teach her any responsibility?"

What a jerk. Cali's been taking care of her sick mom—that's responsibility!

I guess he doesn't speak Mandarin, because my mom answers him in English. "Maybe she say good-bye to her friends."

"Well, we've been waiting for an hour already. Who are her friends? Where do they live?"

Kaigo's fire rises in my throat.

Mr. Chen steps across the porch and calls into Cali's house. "Marnie, come on. Let's drive around the neighborhood and look for her."

"She has friends on Palmer Street," Mom says. "I show you." She goes to get her shoes.

Cali's father paces the porch. "What's the matter with that girl? She knows we want to leave this morning."

I can't take this guy any more. How dare he be mad at Cali when he's the one messing up her life? I slip out onto the porch, check that Mom is out of earshot, and whisper-yell, "What's the matter with *her*? Sir, are you serious? Her mom is sick. She has to move away to live with a dad who doesn't even know who her friends are . . ."

Mr. Chen stops pacing and stares at me.

"Then you show up with a surprise, live-in girlfriend. The question isn't what's wrong with her, it's what's wrong with you!" I take a deep breath and look down at the floorboards. Oh my God, I can't believe I just said that.

He shoots laser death beams at me. "Do you know where she is or not?"

Marnie steps out onto the porch. "Wait, Richard. You didn't tell Cali about me? You told me she was excited to come to Montreal and live with us."

"I meant to tell her."

Still looking down, I see something move under the porch.

"But you didn't. Maybe we need to look at this through Cali's eyes. She's probably just a scared little girl who wants her mom. Ooh, maybe that's where she went—to the hospital. What do you think, Jaden?"

"Maybe," I lie.

Mom comes out the door.

Marnie takes the keys from Cali's father and locks the front door. "Linda, can you show us the way to Cali's friends? If we don't find her there we'll try the hospital."

"Of course. Jaden, you stay here in case Cali come back."

When the three adults drive off in Mr. Chen's blue car, I race down the steps and around the side of the porch. I lift the familiar board and duck into Spy Club.

In the grayness, Cali sits on a tiny chair, her knees pulled up to her chin.

"What's going on?"

"I don't want to go."

"Okay . . . So what's the plan?"

She shrugs. "Hide under the porch till they leave."

"Um . . . is there a backup plan, like for when they call the police?"

She sniffs. "No."

"Alright then." I walk, hunched over, to the chair next to Cali. Have these things gotten smaller? I sit and put my feet up on the little desk.

In the days of Spy Club, we sometimes sat here for hours without talking so we wouldn't give ourselves away. We got pretty good at communicating with only our eyes and hand signals.

I look down at my hands. For once my thumbs are calm. I only wish there was a cheat I could input to improve Mrs. Chen's Health Meter.

Cali breaks the silence. "Thanks for saying that to my dad just now."

"I'm not sure that was a good idea. He seemed pretty pissed."

"So what? I'm pissed too. Everything you said is true."

"What if you just go with them? It's only for a few months, until your mom comes home."

Cali shakes her head. "Last night at dinner my dad said they're making their office into my bedroom. I can paint it whatever color I want."

"Okay . . . What color did you pick?"

"Don't you get it? They're changing their whole house around for me. People don't do that if someone is just visiting. I don't think my mom's telling me the truth. This move is permanent."

"So, you need to talk to your mom."

"Yeah. I wish I could see her before we leave. I'd ask her straight up. She wouldn't be able to look me in the eyes and lie."

"Then let's go to the hospital."

"What's the point? They'll all be there before us, and I won't get to talk to her alone."

"They're stopping at Aliyah and Evy's places first." I look at my watch. "Wait here. I have an idea." I rush into the house. Man, I hope Melanie wakes up in a good mood.

CHAPTER 21

Ten minutes later, Roy pulls up in his little gray hatchback. I introduce him to Cali.

"Thanks for coming so fast." I climb into the back seat.

"No problem. I told you I'd give you a ride to the tournament."

"Actually, we need you to take us to the hospital—"

Cali cuts me off. "Oh my God—the tournament! Jaden, you're going to miss it!"

"It's okay, there's lots of time. Let's get you to your mom first."

"Don't you play at eleven?"

"I'll make it," I say. It's a long shot, but I grabbed the bag with my controller on the way out the door, just in case.

Cali's not buying my fake confidence. "It's already ten fifteen."

Roy looks back at us, his face scrunched up. "So where am I going?"

"Tournament."

"Hospital," I say forcefully, over top of Cali.

"Okay, hospital then tournament. Buckle up."

Me and Cali don't talk on the ride to the hospital—we're too busy hanging on to our seats. Although he never goes over the speed limit, Roy also doesn't slow down when making turns. It's like we're in one of those kart-racing games. I keep waiting for the wheels on one side of the car to lift off the ground when we go around a bend.

"You're lucky," Roy calls over his shoulder. "I won't have this car much longer. I just got accepted to college. I'll be putting this baby up on Craigslist next week to pay for tuition."

"Congrats," I answer through clenched teeth as we take another corner at warp speed.

At 10:26 a.m. the car screeches to a stop in the round driveway by the main entrance to the hospital. Me and Cali get out of opposite doors.

"What are you doing? Go to the tournament."

"Are you sure? I'll come in with you if you want."

Cali looks at her watch. "No. If you go now you might still make it in time."

"Alright. Good luck."

"You too."

I get into the passenger seat this time. Roy hits the gas and we're off like it's a time trial—we really are racing against the clock.

"Which way?" he asks at the exit.

"Turn right. Take the highway."

Roy whips the car onto the main street, and I spy a familiar blue car turning into the hospital parking lot.

"Oh no. That's them."

"Who?"

"We have to go back so I can stall them." I quickly explain the situation, and Roy pulls a kart-driving stunt that spins the car around so fast I'm dizzy. Before I know it, we're back in the circular drive.

"So, your mom's in that blue car? How are you going to explain why you're in my car?"

Oh crap! If this was a kart-racing game, I'd have a bomb to throw out and cause a distraction, but I've got nothing, not even banana peels for them to slip on. "Let me out here by the doors. Hopefully she won't see you."

I jump out of the car and run through the main doors and across the lobby to the elevator. Wait, I don't even know what floor to go to. I spin around, searching for a solution.

The information desk.

I dash over and ask the elderly lady behind the counter for Mrs. Chen's room number. She pats her blue volunteer vest and then her head. "Now, where did I put my glasses?"

"They're on the desk there." I point with a fidgety finger.

"Oh! Thank you. Now, what was the name again?"

"Chen."

"Chen? How do you spell that?"

I try to sound patient as I spell it out. She slowly one-fingers it into the computer and, after a long pause, tells me the room is number 602.

I run for the elevator and get there just as the doors slide shut. I'm frantically pressing the up button when Mom, Cali's father, and Marnie come through the doors from the parking lot.

"*Er zi*, what are you doing here?"

"I found Cali. I brought her here to talk to her mom before she leaves." I look at Cali's father. "I know you're in a rush, but can you please give them some time alone?"

Marnie reaches into her pocket for a tissue and dabs her eyes. "Oh gosh. Of course we can give her time. Right, Richard?"

The elevator doors open and all four of us get in. There's silence until it stops on the sixth floor. We get out and follow my mom.

She speaks brusquely in Mandarin. "What do you mean you brought her here? How did you get here so fast?"

"A friend gave us a ride." That's not a lie.

"What friend of yours can drive?"

I pretend not to hear the question.

We pass room 602 and see Cali sitting on a chair by the bed. I catch her eye and continue to the waiting room next door. We all settle onto vinyl couches under framed paintings of farms in winter.

Marnie sniffs and dabs her eyes again. "How did we not think to check if she wanted to say good-bye to her mom? Oh . . . I'm not going to be a very good mother, am I?"

"Of course you are." Mr. Chen pats Marnie on the arm.

These guys are too weird. I try to bite my tongue, but after exploding at Mr. Chen on the porch I'm kind of on a roll. "Cali has a mom," I mumble. "You're not going to be her mother. Ever."

Beside me, my mom stiffens.

"Oh, I know that dear." Marnie is still dabbing her eyes. "But I *am* going to be a mom soon." She pats her stomach.

Seriously?

"Oh, uh, congratulation," Mom sputters.

"Thank you. I'm really excited." Marnie points to Cali's father. "This one is so calm about it because he's done it all before."

Mom's angry-bull breath tells me she's thinking

the same thing I am: *Only the first few years. Then he took off.*

I look at my watch: 10:43 a.m. I accomplished my mission. How can I get back to Roy and drive to the tournament without answering Mom's question? She will definitely want to know how I got Roy's number.

Cali rushes into the waiting room and straight to me. "What are you doing here? You're never going to make it on time. Go!"

"Oh, the tournament. I forgot." Mom stands up and looks at her watch. "I have no car. I can't take you."

Cali looks at me. I shake my head slightly to keep her quiet.

Her father interrupts. "Cali. What were you thinking, taking off this morning? This kind of behavior is completely unacceptable."

Marnie puts a hand on Mr. Chen's shoulder to quiet him. Then she looks at Cali. "Honey, are you okay?"

"Yeah, what did your mom say?" I ask.

"She . . . uh . . ." Cali looks around at everyone in the waiting room, then speaks to me. "She just doesn't know for sure." She presses her lips together, and her voice goes to a higher pitch. "She thinks it'll be too hard for me to take care of her and go to school. That's why she called my dad. So I can get used to living with him, in case . . ."

"You were right then?"

Cali nods.

"What do you mean?" Mom asks.

"Cali isn't just going to Montreal for a little while. She's going to be staying there. Maybe forever."

Cali looks at her father. "Jaden's going to miss the most important event of his life if he doesn't leave, like, right now. Dad, can you please drive him to the tournament?"

"What? No, Cali, I think I should talk to your mother—"

Marnie interjects. "Richard, Jaden is Cali's friend, and he's been taking care of her. We should take him."

"It's okay. I can take him."

All eyes turn to the doorway.

CHAPTER 22

"Roy? What you doing here?" Mom blinks rapidly. "Everything okay?"

"Everything's fine, Mrs. Stiles. I drove Jaden and Cali here. I was waiting outside and looking at the clock and . . . well, if Jaden is going to compete we really need to get moving."

"Mom?"

"Okay, let's go."

Marnie looks at Cali. "You probably want to watch him play, right, sweetheart?"

"Well, yeah, I'd love to"—she looks at her father—"if I could."

"We can leave this afternoon, right, Richard?"

Cali's father takes a deep breath. Marnie nods her head slowly. He sighs. "Go. But we're leaving as soon as it's over."

Cali gives her father a hug. Then she turns to Marnie and gives her a timid one too. "Thank you," she says, more to Marnie than her father.

The clock in Roy's hatchback shows 10:55 a.m. by the time we are all buckled up. Roy's driving style shifts significantly with my mom in the passenger seat. Instead of turning like he's in a NASCAR race, he putt-putts along like he's driving a golf cart.

We're never going to make it.

"How you know Jaden need a ride to the hospital?"

Roy ignores the question and steers the conversation in another direction. "I have good news and bad news to share with you, Mrs. Stiles." She looks at him, and he takes it as a sign to continue. "The bad news is I'm going to have to cut back on my shifts at the diner this fall. The good news is I was accepted into the social service worker program I applied to."

"What is a social service worker?"

"I want to be a youth counselor and run programs for teens who are having problems. If they have a safe place to hang out and someone to talk to they're less likely to get involved with drugs and gangs."

Mom looks out the window and is quiet for a moment. Then she looks back at Roy and says, "This is a very important job. Melanie is lucky."

Roy's wide eyes catch mine in the rearview mirror.

Mom laughs. "You think I not know?"

"Um, well, I . . ."

"Oh, I know long time now. But girls don't want to date a boy their mother like. So I think, better if Melanie not know I like you."

◄○►

Roy pulls the car up in front of the hotel at 11:13 a.m. I jump out and sprint through the lobby, following the T3 signs with Cali right behind me.

At the sign-in table I skid to a halt and, gasping for breath, say, "I'm Jaden Stiles. JStar. I'm late. Did I miss it?"

"JStar? They were calling for you. Sorry, by not showing at the station you forfeited your first match."

"Oh no. Jaden, I'm so sorry," Cali says.

"Wait. Just the first match? I'm still in, right? The rules say it's a double-elimination bracket."

"Right. That loss bumps you down to the loser bracket. Now if you lose any match you're out."

Not quite the odds I had hoped for, but I'll take it.

The guy gives me some papers and a competitor's pass attached to a yellow lanyard. I loop it around my neck and push open the conference room door.

In the center of the huge room, rows of chairs face a large screen on one wall. This is where the highlighted battles are being projected and live-streamed for all to see. Along the other three walls are numbered stations, each set up with two chairs facing a monitor.

The hype is unreal. It's so crowded it's hard to get through. Matches for several different games are underway, and spectators stop here and there to watch, blocking the flow of traffic. Every few seconds a crowd around a screen calls out a collective "Oh!" in reaction to a great hit. The air in the room is heavy from the heat of all the machines and smells a bit like a guys' locker room.

I grip the schedule in my left hand. It says my next match starts in fifteen minutes against someone with the gamertag WarpSpeed.

"You okay?" Cali asks.

"No. I'm freaking out. I don't see anyone my age here. I didn't know there would be so many OGs."

"OG? What's that mean? Old guys?"

"It stands for Original Generation. Some of these guys have been playing *Cross Ups* since it first came out."

"When was that?"

"Like, before we were born." I shrug my backpack off and deflate into a seat in the back row. Instead of feeling like Yuudai Sato, ready to battle anyone, I feel like a little kid at an NHL game watching the pros play. Man, I even have my parents with me. "This is going to be so embarrassing."

Cali sits down beside me. "Don't worry. Just have fun. Hey, isn't that Hugh?"

I catch a glimpse of Hugh and wave him over. Then I lose sight of him as he makes his way through the crowd. When he finally gets to us, Devesh peeks out from behind him.

"What? I thought you were grounded."

"I whined so much about missing the tournament that my dad gave in and let me go."

Hugh moves to block Devesh from talking to me. "Dude, where have you been? They called you so many times."

Devesh squishes past Hugh. "I almost pretended to be you and played your first match."

"But I wouldn't let him. I knew you'd get here. Why are you so late?"

"It's a long story."

Devesh catches my I-don't-want-to-talk-about-it look and changes the subject. "Have you seen the controllers these guys have?" His eyes follow a competitor carrying a large plastic box with the *Cross*

Ups logo across the top. "It looks like they ripped off the front of an arcade game."

"Yeah, those arcade sticks are bananas," Hugh says.

"Um . . . You guys are not helping." Cali chops her hand back and forth in front of her throat. "I was just telling Jaden not to get stressed out."

"Oh yeah, J, you're gonna do great," Hugh says.

"Thanks, Hughie. I just hope this doesn't turn out to be an epic fail."

CHAPTER 23

My opponent is already seated and staring at the screen when I get to the station. I put my bag on the chair and get out my game pad. It suddenly feels so tiny in my hands.

WarpSpeed moves a bulky arcade stick from his lap and gets up to face me, hand outstretched. I'm surprised to recognize him as the Trekkie from the comic book store.

"Hey, kid. Let's see if you can boldly go where no one has gone before."

"Uh, okay."

The Trekkie sits back down and points to the console. "Engage."

I fumble to plug my controller in and sit down.

Devesh puts his hands on my shoulders. "You can do it, Jaden. Just pretend you're Yuudai Sato. Be Yuudai."

"Shut up, dude. Remember what happened when you told him, 'Be Joshua'? He doesn't need to be anyone else. He's freakin' amazing." Hugh pushes Devesh aside to stand next to me. He looks me in the eyes, all intense. "Just play like you always do."

Cali agrees. "You've got this."

I select Kaigo. My opponent choses Cantu and a calm comes over me. The matchup couldn't get any better. It'll be just like playing against Josh at home.

As soon as the *FIGHT* sign flashes, I try my bread-and-butter combo, but my crouching light punch is blocked. The Trekkie jumps up for an overhead attack, kicking me in the face repeatedly.

Click click click.

As I take some damage, I hear WarpSpeed hitting the buttons on his controller. Man, that thing is loud. What a total giveaway. This guy likes to be in the air, and I know exactly when he's going up.

I stay upright now. When I hear the next series of rapid clicks I throw a flip kick and punish the Trekkie. *Yeah, you can go up there, but you're coming down hard.*

I try my favorite combo again and land it easily. I land six fireballs in a row and watch my opponent

and his Health Meter melt. A final uppercut and the
screen flashes *K.O.*

I smile and take a second to look up. In the mirrors on the wall I see the reflection of the crowded
room behind me. My friends are smiling, but it's my
mom's reaction I really want to see. She looks con-
fused, but not upset. Dad has arrived, and he's pointing to the monitor, explaining what just happened.

The rest of the match is easy. I listen for the
sounds of my opponent hitting buttons for attacks
and use that information to block or counterattack.
My fireballs keep Cantu on the defense so her neck
never divides into snakes. I use my Dragon Tail
Super to swipe her right off the screen.

"Fascinating." The Trekkie raises an eyebrow,
shakes my hand, and unplugs. "Live long and pros-
per, kid."

"Thanks." I hope all my matches are like this.

I turn around to face my parents.

"You sure made quick work of that guy, son."

"I think he's more into *Star Trek* than *Cross Ups*."

"You win easy."

I look at my mom, waiting to see if she'll say
more.

She notices my questioning look. "I still don't

like this game," she continues, but her smile shows she doesn't hate it either.

—◄o►—

In a way, it's not so bad that I missed my first match. Being in the loser bracket makes the tournament easier because everyone I play has already lost a match. The real superstars are all in the winner bracket.

In my next matches I battle a bunch of casual gamers. None of them came here to win, but they all look a bit bummed to get kicked out by someone my age. One guy obviously just came to the tournament to hang out with his friends, a bunch of skinny guys who look just like him, all wearing black hoodies and jeans. They stand behind him and laugh as he loses every round to me. In the last round I even pull off a perfect—I don't take any damage at all. It's almost too easy.

I'm in the zone, until I sit down beside my next opponent. He's huge, like the kind of guy you'd expect to find on a football field instead of playing video games. I think he's bigger than the yeti-cross he's playing. He has an arcade stick controller, but it looks tiny in his lap. I try to use the sound of his buttons to help me, but the crowd is getting louder, and that makes listening for attacks harder. He's good, and he destroys me in the first game. I hear him talking about pulling an all-nighter gaming with his pals to prepare. I guess that means he's tired, because he makes some stupid mistakes, and I take advantage of them to win the second and third games.

After the match, he reaches out to shake my hand. I hesitate. Everyone shakes hands after games here, but he looks mad and his hand is huge. I'm worried he'll crush mine. When he leans in, I'm sure he's going to tell me off. Instead, he breaks into a smile. "Good game, li'l man. I'm gonna keep my eye on you."

Between matches I notice some OGs chatting with my parents. Every time I look over, my mom's talking to someone new. Sometimes she's even smiling.

Me and Cali walk the room, waiting for my next match. My eyes flick from left to right, trying to take it all in. There's so much to see, and I don't want to miss anything.

Cali yawns. "These guys look like robots. Don't they have any emotions?"

I look at the two players battling in front of us. Both have totally blank expressions. In fact, if it weren't for their hands moving at lightning speed over their controllers, I'd think they were daydreaming.

"Just because they don't show it doesn't mean they don't feel anything." I turn to Cali. "When I'm playing, I feel so many things, but it doesn't show on my face or in my words." I pause. "Actually, I'm like that in real life too."

Cali smiles. "Guess it's a boy thing."

"Hey, there are girls here too."

"True. There are a total of twelve females in this room, including your mom and me. I counted."

She's got a point. All of my competitors are guys.

For my next match, a huge crowd has gathered around my station. I hear someone say, "You gotta see this little kid with the big moves."

The guy I'm battling, Mr_Burns, is OG. He looks very serious when he shakes my hand. "Listen, I'm not going to go easy on you because you're a kid," he says. He's a big guy, and he's sweating through his *Simpsons* T-shirt.

He plays Lerus, who I've always thought is the weakest character, but he sure knows how to make the best of her. We go round for round, neither of us taking two rounds in a row. He wins game one; I win game two. We're tied in game three, one round each. If this pattern continues, Mr_Burns will have the victory.

I stop myself from looking at the mirrors because the huge crowd in the reflection freaks me out. I focus on the screen.

As soon as the *FIGHT* sign disappears, he grabs me and throws me. I jump up and over Lerus to work my favorite combo from behind. The cross up works! I add a few fireballs, and his Health Meter sinks.

My next block is too slow because I'm checking my Super Meter. Lerus's powerful horse kicks bring my health down halfway. As soon as I can, I go for the Dragon Breath Super and breathe fire all over Lerus.

It's so close. While I'm waiting for my Super Meter to refill, I throw a frenzy of fireballs that all whiff. I'm panicking.

For her Super, Lerus transforms into a unicorn and gallops at me, head bowed so her glittering horn can make contact. Just before she spears me, I leap up and land on her, laying a jab combo into her

horselike back. She topples. I take advantage of the hit stun and throw my Dragon Breath Super. There's no missing from here.

K.O.

Yes! This win puts me into the semi-finals. Two more wins and I have two thousand dollars.

Mr_Burns gets up. "You're one to watch, kid," he says as he gives me a big sweaty handshake.

Random people in the crowd give me high fives as I leave the station. Before I can get very far, Hugh and Devesh tackle me. Sweat runs down the sides of Hugh's pink face. "We just checked the bracket. You're playing on the live-stream next—"

"—against Kn1ght_Rage," Devesh finishes.

CHAPTER 24

Hearing Kn1ght_Rage's name makes my stomach flip.

"You beat him before. You can do it again." Hugh's smile is bigger than his face.

"But I still don't know how I did that Super. It was a button mash. Plus, I'm not so good at blocking his Solar Burst, and he knows it now. He can deplete my meter so fast . . ."

Cali cuts me off. "Then you'll beat him some other way."

"Has anyone seen this guy? Is he OG or our age or what?" Devesh scans the room.

Hugh jumps right into spy mode. "We've got half an hour. Let's figure out who he is. Maybe that will give you an edge."

"I'm too nervous to look."

"You go sit in the lobby and chill a bit," Devesh says. "We'll run the recon mission."

"Let's split up to cover more ground. We'll meet by Jaden in twenty minutes." Hugh starts weaving his way through the crowd. Cali walks off in the other direction, and Devesh follows her.

In the lobby I find a couch, lean back, and close my eyes, trying to think about anything except the upcoming battle with Kn1ght_Rage.

A minute later, Mom sits down next to me. "Are you having fun, *er zi*?"

"I'm too scared to have fun."

Her face tenses. "What's wrong?"

I change to Mandarin since that worked better the other day. "Nothing. Why do you always worry so much?"

The deep breath she takes is not an angry-bull breath. She sounds more like a tired animal that just finished a long journey. "When I was your age, my older brother Li Yun made bad decisions. He chose a violent lifestyle. I worry you will do the same if I don't keep you safe."

"What do you mean?"

She lets out another tired breath. "Where we grew up there were many gangs. My mother tried hard to keep us kids away, but Li Yun was drawn to the idea of having power over people. My mother

was so worried, she even spent her limited money
to buy us each some jade to wear. In Chinese culture, they say the jade stone can protect you from
harm."

I look down at the green bracelet she never
takes off.

She follows my gaze. "Yes, she gave me this bracelet. And she gave each of my brothers a jade ring."

"But it didn't work to protect Li Yun."

"On the day he was killed, Li Yun left his ring at
home, so who knows? I think maybe it would have
protected him. I still keep it with me to remember
him." She pulls a small red pouch from her purse
and opens it to reveal a pale green ring.

"Couldn't you just give us all some jade to wear?
Then you won't worry so much."

"Actually, I did."

I think about this. "Melanie and Josh's pendants,
right?"

She nods.

I can't think of any green jewelry I own. "And
me? You just try to stop me from seeing anything
violent? Why didn't you give me some jade too?"

"Sometimes you are so smart, and sometimes
you miss the obvious. You can have Li Yun's ring"—

she places it in my hand—"but you don't need it. I named you Jaden so you will always have jade with you." Mom cups my face in her hands and looks into my eyes. "Your name is not something you can leave at home."

A warmth rushes over me.

"You know, *er zi*, you look a lot like Li Yun."

"Is that why you worry so much about me? I'm not like him, you know."

"I know. When your teacher said you chose not to fight, I was so proud of you. Your actions show what kind of person you really are."

I want to give her a hug, but then I remember where we are.

Dad crosses the lobby to join us. "Well, son, you are certainly the talk of the room. One of the organizers told me that they're getting a lot of requests to see you play on the streaming, whatever that means."

"Great. That means my whole school will be watching my next match."

Mom says, "You know, I am very surprise. People here so friendly."

"We were expecting something different." Dad pulls open his jacket to reveal a black T-shirt with the letters *GDLK* printed in white. "Look, they even sell these great T-shirts that say *Good Luck*."

I cover my face with my hands. "Please tell me you're joking."

"Why?"

I sigh. "Dad, *GDLK* means godlike, not good luck."

"Oh. Well, it's still a very nice crowd. And it looks like you're holding your own in there. When's your next match?"

"Soon."

"Did you eat something?" Mom asks.

"Nah, I'm too nervous. I'll eat after."

"You need to eat. I'll get you something." With that she rushes off in the direction of the hotel restaurant.

Hugh is the first to report back. "Not sure where Kn1ght_Rage is. Someone said he went for lunch."

Devesh arrives a minute later, with no news. "Nice shirt, Mr. Stiles."

I get up to put the ring in my pocket and see Cali coming back with a big smile on her face.

"I just met Kn1ght_Rage," she reports. "He's a total OG—balding and kinda chubby, but really friendly. He told me to tell you good luck."

"See, son? Good luck!" Dad points to his T-shirt. "Nothing to worry about. He's a nice guy."

"And I think he knows your mom," Cali continues. "They're chatting in the restaurant right now."

"What? Mom knows a gamer?" I look at Dad, who just shrugs.

A few minutes later, I climb the steps to the stage in front of the big screen. I plug in and take a seat with my back to the rows of chairs. A few people call out, "Good luck, kid," and I hear my father's voice join the mix. I hope he's not pointing to his T-shirt again.

My thumbs tap away at the tiny controller in my hands. I think of my uncle's jade ring in my pocket and close my eyes. Just gotta be myself.

"So, we finally get to battle in person, JStar."

I recognize the voice, but I don't believe my ears until I open my eyes and see the familiar face looking down at me.

CHAPTER 25

When I stand up to shake my competitor's hand, my mouth is hanging open so wide I could probably swallow my controller.

From the crowd I hear Hugh call, "Oh my God!" followed by murmurs as people clue in that I'm about to take on my math teacher.

"Surprise!" Mr. Efram says. "I was tempted to reveal myself to you a few times this week, but that look on your face was definitely worth the wait."

"*You're* Kn1ght_Rage?"

"Yup. And I'm about to show you how we OGs battle."

I'm so dead.

I sit down and select Kaigo. I see that Mr. Efram selected Blaze. My heart hammers in my chest, competing with my nervous thumbs on the controller.

The screen flashes *FIGHT.*

I start on the defensive, back dashing and blocking. As soon as my opponent's Super Meter is full, I crouch to block any Solar Burst Supers. But he throws a different Super, Solar Flame, where he flies overhead dropping fiery feathers. Since I'm crouched, my block doesn't work and I take full damage.

I try my bread-and-butter combo, but Blaze juggles Kaigo and throws him like a candy-bar wrapper. The crowd boos. I back dash some more and crouch again, to block any Solar Bursts.

I get hit over and over with basic kicks and punches. I spend so much time in a crouched defensive position that my opponent stays in the air, so my crouch block won't work.

This is sad. He doesn't even need his Solar Burst to take me down.

I'm going to lose if I don't take a chunk of his life. I try desperately to play Kaigo's Super, but my timing is off.

One last flying side kick hits me in the jaw.

K.O.

The second round is almost identical to the first. When I'm knocked out, Kn1ght_Rage's Health Meter is almost full. I hardly touched him.

Well, that's game one. Why is he beating me with basics? When's he going to throw Solar Burst?

The second game is a bit better. I get Kaigo's Dragon Breath Super to hit Blaze twice, and come close to winning the second round. Unfortunately, I back dash into a corner, and Blaze goes ham on me with some basic chain combos.

K.O.

What a sad way to go out. The crowd boos again, and I crumple inside.

I look over at Mr. Efram. He's shaking his left hand and wincing, but his right hand is still holding his controller and he's not getting up. He's getting ready to play another game.

That's when I remember the rule sheet. It's three out of five in the semis and finals.

This thing isn't over yet.

CHAPTER 26

I stare at Mr. Efram. It's so weird to be battling my math teacher. I picture him in class, pointing his thumb at the stupid USAR problem-solving poster.

I shake my head. Focus! This isn't math class. This is the most important battle of my life. I'm going to totally embarrass myself in front of everyone watching if I don't find a way to pull this off.

I can't sit here forever. I have to start the next game. Everyone's waiting.

But I've got nothing but that dumb poster in my head.

I guess it can't hurt. I mean, if I understand my opponent better, maybe I can find a way to beat him.

Step 1: Understand.

What do I know about Mr. Efram? He likes math . . . he collects comics . . . he sweats a lot . . . This is not helping. Aaah!

Okay, what do I know about Kn1ght_Rage? He likes to use Solar Burst . . . but he hasn't used it yet. Why?

Next to me, Mr. Efram is massaging his left hand. I remember yesterday when he yelled "Son of a Borg" and realize he can't throw Solar Burst— his hand hurts too much from banging on the window latch in class.

Step 2: Strategize.

I know exactly what to do. Stop defending against the Solar Burst—it's not coming.

Step 3: Attack.

I press start and go on the attack. Instead of back dashing and blocking, I hammer Blaze.

The crowd likes my new aggressive style and screams whenever I land a good hit. I stay away from the Dragon Breath Super since I always get thrown. Instead, I use fireball combos and add a lot of anti air. I win four of the next six rounds to take games three and four.

It's all tied up. The crowd goes crazy.

Game on.

In round one of the final game, I try the Dragon Fire Super as soon as my meter is full. The crowd groans when nothing happens.

How the heck did I do it that day? I don't get it.

I go back to the problem-solving steps.

Step 1: Understand.

What's different? I mean, I wasn't even thinking that day. Maybe that's it.

Step 2: Strategize.

I need to relax and stop thinking so hard about each move.

Step 3: Attack.

Let's do this! I back dash and wait for an opening.

Wait . . . wait . . . now. I try not to think about the combination of buttons and stick positions.

Nothing.

Mr. Efram grunts in pain and plays Solar Burst before I can react. I take hard punishment. In a panic I try Dragon Fire again. Nothing happens again. The crowd groans again. On screen, Blaze tosses Kaigo and I'm K.O.

Mr. Efram lets go of the controller, winces, and shakes his left hand a few times. If he wins another round it's over.

I realize I'm missing a step.

Step 4: Reflect.

The only time Dragon Fire has worked was that one time I wasn't thinking about it. But how can I do that in the middle of this game?

Someone in the crowd yells, "Come on, kid." A few others join in with calls of encouragement, but one voice sticks out. "You can do it, son."

I turn around to see Dad, standing proudly in the front row. Next to him, Cali catches my eye. She holds out her hands, slowly pushing them down three times. I know what she means—relax. I think of the game Cali's mom taught her for falling asleep. It's worth a try.

The next time Kaigo's Super Meter is full, I name comic book characters. *A* . . . Aquaman . . . *B* . . . Batman . . . *C* . . . Catwoman . . .

I nail a Dragon Fire Super. It's working!

D . . . Daredevil . . . *E* . . . Elektra . . . *F* . . . Flash Gordon—hey, that's *F* and *G*!

Gray smoke!

A minute later: *H* . . . Hulk . . . *I* . . . Iron Man . . . *J* . . . What starts with *J*? Oh, Joker!

More smoke.

K.O.

There is a collective "Oooooh!" from the audience,

and the energy in the room is over the top. If I win the last round, I'm in the finals!

Now that I've got the Dragon Fire Super working, Kaigo spends more time in dragon form than human form. Whenever my Super Meter is full I scroll through the alphabet and the dragon spins across the screen. I'm on the easiest letter—*S* for Superman—when Blaze hits the ground for the last time.

K.O.

Everyone goes wild, hooting and pointing at the stage. Hugh, Devesh, and Cali give each other high fives. Even Mom gets up from her seat and claps wildly.

Mr. Efram reaches out his right hand. "Congratulations, Jaden. I thought I had you, but obviously you had a few tricks up your sleeve."

I shake his hand. "Thanks, but it wasn't really a fair match." I point to his other hand. "We should have a rematch when your thumb is better and you can use Solar Burst without crying."

He looks down at his left hand. "Yeah, that really hurt. But if you figured out my weakness, you deserve the win."

CHAPTER 27

I am mobbed by my friends and family.

"You made the final!" Devesh raises my arm in victory.

"You really did well under all that pressure, son." Hugh rushes over from checking the bracket. "Jaden, you play Umehara in the final."

"That is the boy who won last year and the year before."

The whole group turns and looks at my mom.

"What? I talk to people." She shrugs and we all laugh. Then she looks at me. "You can beat him?"

"Probably not. I still can't believe I beat Kn1ght_ Rage . . . I mean Mr. E . . . man, that was so weird." I shake my head.

Mom pulls a hamburger from a paper bag. "Here."

"*Xie xie, Ma ma.*" I thank her.

◄○►

I step onto the stage fifteen minutes later full of confidence. I beat my nemesis Kn1ght_Rage. I know how to relax and land Dragon Fire. Only one match stands between me and victory.

There's so much hype in the room, and I know more people are watching at home. The energy fills me up.

Umehara is on the young side, probably eighteen or nineteen. His shaggy hair is tucked up under a black baseball hat he's wearing backward. His purple T-shirt has *Twitch* written across it. He's probably sponsored by them. I shake his hand and plug in my controller.

He selects Saki. Alright, I can do this. Just like playing Cali.

The *FIGHT* sign flashes.

I try my go-to combo. It's blocked and I get thrown. Before I'm out of hit stun, Umehara is into his next attack. Everything is a blur. It only takes about ten seconds for all my confidence to drain, just like my Health Meter.

I feel like a noob. This must be what Devesh and Hugh feel like when they play against me. Umehara's rushdown is so fast it's impossible to keep up. All my fireballs miss and my blocks come too late. I try over and over to relax and hit Dragon Fire, but I never even come close. I'm so dizzy I can't get past the letter *A* in the alphabet.

Totally dominated.

The match lasts no time, and I don't win a single round.

When the final *K.O.* flashes on the screen, I breathe deeply through my nose, almost like the angry bull.

But I'm not angry; I'm trying not to cry.

Why'd I ever think I could win? I'm such a fraud.

I shake Umehara's hand and unplug without looking up.

An announcer jumps onto the stage and turns us to face the spectators. I don't want to see Cali. I let her down. No money, no ramp. She's really going.

The announcer speaks into his microphone. "I'm pleased to announce our second-place player in *Cross Ups IV*, a young man who has become a crowd favorite today, Jaden Stiles."

He raises my hand above my head, but I keep looking down.

The crowd hoots and chants, "JStar, JStar." My face gets hot as the chant gets louder and faster.

When it finally dies out and the announcer presents the grand prize to Umehara, the clapping is polite, but far less energetic.

They really wanted me to win!

◄o►

It doesn't seem to matter that I lost. As I walk through the conference room, people give me high fives and clap me on the back.

I feel like the champion of the tournament.

A guy in his twenties approaches us with his hand out. He's wearing a black toque and a red T-shirt with the name *ArcadeStix*, where the *X* is made out of two sticks of wood.

"Hi there, sir. Ma'am." He shakes hands energetically with both of my parents. "I wonder if I could have a minute of your family's time."

"Okay," Dad says.

"My name's Kyle Obren. I work for ArcadeStix." He points to his shirt with one hand and hands Mom a business card with the other. "We're one of the sponsors for this event."

"Yes, I see your signs everywhere," Mom says.

"That's us." He turns to me. "Anyway, we also sponsor a team of gamers. They're the guys you see around here in these red shirts. After watching you play today, I think you'd make a great addition to our team. I'd love to see what you could do with one of our products in your hands."

"What does this mean?" Mom asks.

"We want to sponsor your son. If Jaden joins our team, we'll give him an ArcadeStix product to practice with. Then, we'll pay his entrance fees for tournaments and send him out to represent us. He keeps any money he wins."

OMG, that's my dream . . .

"And what's in it for you?" Dad raises an eyebrow.

"Fair question. Honestly, I think Jaden could be the next big player on the circuit. He got a lot of attention here today. The guys at the streaming table never had so many hits before. And attention is what ArcadeStix wants. If everyone is watching Jaden play, we want them to see him using our product and wearing our logo." He points to his T-shirt again.

"I don't know." Mom shakes her head. "He has school. This tournament is his first try."

"That's the amazing thing. But this won't affect school. The tournaments are always on weekends, and you control how many he attends." Kyle smiles. "Listen, you don't have to decide this instant. Just think about it." He turns back to me and gives me a fist bump. "Amazing battles today, kid. Godlike!"

CHAPTER 28

I'm surrounded by people who want to talk to me. Devesh and Hugh help me handle all the questions.

"Jaden is our best bud," Hugh says.

"Oh, yeah," Devesh joins in, "we play together all the time."

My ears perk up when someone asks, "Are you guys as good as him?"

"Almost," Devesh brags.

I glance over to see Hugh elbow Devesh.

"But this girl's amazing," Devesh says, pointing to Cali. "She's the next one to watch."

Mr. Efram strides through the crowd. "Look who showed up just in time to watch Jaden play the finals." He looks over his shoulder at Ty and Flash, who trail behind him. "I'm so glad you boys are all getting along again."

Mr. Efram turns to talk with my parents, leaving Ty and Flash rolling their eyes.

"Pff," Ty puffs. "I knew you wouldn't win."

"Um, didn't you see my man totally school Mr. E?" Devesh pats me on the back.

"What? Mr. E was playing?" Flash says.

"Um, yeah," Hugh says. "It was epic."

Flash looks at Ty. "I can't believe we missed that."

"Whatever," Ty says.

"Anyway," I say. "I want to thank you guys for putting up that banner. If you hadn't told the whole school to watch me play, ArcadeStix wouldn't have asked to sponsor me."

"For real? You got sponsored?" Flash asks.

"Who cares?" Ty pulls Flash by the arm. "Let's go."

"And it's all thanks to you guys," I say as they leave.

I hear Flash say, "That's cool, man. He's our age and he got sponsored."

Ty punches him in the arm. "Shut up."

The moment I've been dreading comes way too fast. Me and Cali stand on the porch.

"It's only six weeks until summer holidays," I say.

My parents convinced Cali's mom and dad to let her spend part of the summer at our place so she can see her mom. They're going to see how Mrs. Chen is doing at the end of the summer and then decide if Cali can go to Layton with me in September.

"I really wish I'd won the money today so I could buy a ramp for you guys. You know, your mom actually helped me at the tournament."

Cali raises an eyebrow.

"I used her alphabet game to help me relax so I could hit Dragon Fire."

"No way! I'm going to tell her that. She'll be glad she was a part of things." She turns to pick up her duffel bag from the porch swing.

"Wait."

She turns back.

"I . . . um . . . have something for you." I dig in my pocket and pull out my uncle's ring. It slips from my sweaty fingers, lands on the porch, and rolls. I scramble after it. Just as I reach out, it disappears between two boards.

"No!" I run down the steps and push through the

bushes and the loose board. "Oh crap, oh crap!" I crawl on the dirt, searching for the small object in the darkness.

Cali follows me into Spy Club and crouches beside me. "I think it dropped over there." She points to the desk and chairs.

I look over and spot the ring next to one of the tiny chair legs. Thank God!

I pick it up and blow on it to clean it off. Then I hold it out to Cali. "Here. Take this. It might keep you safe . . . or something." Or something? I'm such a loser.

She takes it from me. In her hand it suddenly looks humongous. She slips it onto her thumb and stares at it. "Thanks."

"Jade is for protection. It was my uncle's. He's dead now." Shut up, Jaden.

When she looks up at me she's half laughing, but I see a sparkle of tears in her eyes. "I'm going to miss you."

Her lips touch my cheek for the best nanosecond of my life.

K.O.

ACKNOWLEDGMENTS

Jaden was born at a Writescape workshop, so I will start by thanking these incredible teachers. When I first dipped my toes into the writing ocean, Ruth Walker's encouraging words gave me the confidence to plunge in. Gwynn Scheltema helped me swim through various drafts and Heather O'Connor threw me life lines to navigate the currents.

Thanks to Ted Staunton, whose wonderful Writing for Children classes forced me to write the first chapters and taught me the value of a good critique group.

I am privileged to be part of the Writers' Community of Durham Region, whose members have supported me in many ways; most importantly, they made me say, "I'm a writer," out loud.

To my amazing WIP group—Karen Cole, Heather Tucker, Sandra Clarke, Patrick Meade, Anne MacLachlan, and Steve Chatterton. Thank you for sharing your fantastic stories with me and for helping me breathe fire into my story.

A huge thanks to everyone who read an early version of *Tournament Trouble*: Katharina Benning, Louise Butt, Edmund Chien, Marie Prins, Andrea Adair-Tippins , and Justin Gormley. You each helped to make this novel stronger.

Tournament Trouble was written for my students, particularly the ones who love video games more than books. Thank you to Rawl Chan for patiently playing a newb online. Thanks to Nicholas Victoria for answering all my questions and for calling on his crew at

Basement Gaming to help. Jason Das, Brandon Smith, Chris Tapper, and M.E. Girard, thanks for reading gaming scenes and making them better.

I am grateful to CANSCAIP and its many volunteers. In particular, I appreciate the work that goes into The Writing for Children Competition, which launched *Cross Ups* into the publishing world.

Thank you to my agent, Amy Tompkins, for her guidance.

Heartfelt gratitude to the team at Annick Press, especially my editor, Katie Hearn, who helped me polish *Tournament Trouble*. Also my talented illustrator, Connie Choi, who took the characters I imagined and made them real.

Enormous thanks to my parents for so much support. From reading drafts to babysitting so I could write, without your encouragement my book dream would not have come true.

Finally, to Edward, thank you for not only supporting me, but pushing me to do what I love. I hope by reaching for my dreams I am teaching our children to reach for their own.

annick press
toronto + berkeley

CHAPTER 1

On screen, my dragon-cross, Kaigo, is locked in battle with Saki, the yeti-cross.

Kaigo breathes fire, but before he can melt the ice off Saki's beard, Saki thrusts a snowstorm my way. The fire extinguishes, and Saki comes in for the punishment.

I'm playing my favourite game, *Cross Ups IV*. Kaigo's my main. I play him so much it's like he's a part of me. Not the real me, of course. I'm just a skinny twelve-year-old who's never been in a real fight. Kaigo's the guy I am inside my head.

Kaigo wears kung fu gear and he's totally buff. He's super confident, probably because he can turn into a dragon and blow his opponents' heads off with fireballs.

Most of the time.

Right now, he's being shut down by Saki, who just unleashed a blizzard of punches. The yeti-cross is being played by my friend, Cali. It's the second week of summer holidays and we're playing online.

Cali's gotten good at *Cross Ups* since she moved to live with her dad in Montreal a few months ago. I mean, she was always good, but now she's actually coming close to beating me. I'd better power up.

I go to throw my Dragon Fire Super but she's faster. Her character transforms into a huge yeti and stomps across the screen. Ice flies everywhere. My Health Meter is down to a thin beat of red.

Not cool.

I jump in the air to breathe fire down her neck—a move she never blocks fast enough. But today she does. Before I compute what just happened, a yeti headbutt takes me down.

K.O.

She beat me?

That's not supposed to happen.

Hermlone	Tuesday , 4:08 pm
YES! FINALLY! GTG	

We've been playing for six hours, but I totally don't want to stop. Not on a loss.

JStar   Tuesday , 4:09 pm
1 MORE

Hermlone   Tuesday , 4:09 pm
CAN'T

JStar   Tuesday , 4:09 pm
Y NOT?

Hermlone   Tuesday , 4:10 pm
TRBL TTYL

JStar   Tuesday , 4:10 pm
WHAT KIND OF TRBL?

She logs off before I hit send.

It's not like Cali to run off just because she finally got a win. Is her dad mad at her for playing so long? Or is it something more serious?

Sometimes Cali's like the yeti. She freezes me out.

Sylv Chiang is a middle grade teacher by day and a writer of middle grade fiction by night. She lives in Pickering, Ontario.

Connie Choi graduated from the bachelor of illustration program at Sheridan College. She lives in Toronto, Ontario.